Can Bethany ever have  Joshua?

"Bethany, I told you once that I thanked God for the beating that left me here and brought you to me." He stopped and stood quietly, not looking at Bethany or forcing her to look at him.

Bethany waited. Was he trying to tell her gently that she must forget him? As he didn't add anything further, she dropped his hand and started again to walk off. She didn't want to hear the rest of what he would say. She only wanted to get someplace where she could be alone to cry.

He watched her move off and made no attempt to stop her.

Bethany plunged ahead, her tears blotting out any sight of the lane where she was walking, only anxious to get to the road and, as soon as possible, up to her cabin.

A sudden gust of cold wind slapped against her face. It seemed to shut off her breath and turn her tears to ice. The chill of it on her face added to her mental distress, became physical pain.

Automatically, she pulled her cape tightly about her shoulders and turned away from it. And found herself looking at Joshua, standing with bowed head before the church.

She didn't stop to think whether his feelings for her had changed or not. Only that he was alone and needed comfort. She turned and ran back.

MARY LOUISE COLLN has written many short stories, articles, and poetry. She lives in Tennessee where she can be close to some of her grandchildren. *Falling Water Valley* is Mary's first historical novel.

Books by Mary Louise Colln

HEARTSONG PRESENTS
HP26—Mountain House
HP141—A Place for Love

August 1997

Mary Louise Colln

Falling Water
Valley

Mary Louise Colln

Diana — Remembering
Scotland — and
New Friends
Love
Louise

Heartsong Presents

To Mike,
who walks on higher mountains,
clearer trails.

A note from the Author:
I love to hear from my readers! You may write to me at
the following address: **Mary Louise Colln**
Author Relations
P.O. Box 719
Uhrichsville, OH 44683

ISBN 1-57748-068-6

FALLING WATER VALLEY

Cover illustration by Peter Pagano.

PRINTED IN THE U.S.A.

one

My Dearest Daughter,
I have written you numerous letters and have received none from you, leading me to believe that you have failed to receive mine, since I know you would write me if you knew where to direct the letters.

So I will try once again to get a letter through to you and tell you where I am.

I often think of the day, now more than a year ago, that I left you and that beautiful valley we had at last learned to call home. In the time since then, I have never regretted my decision to use my medical skills for the Confederate Army instead of the Union, even though I am opposed to slavery. The need is as great here as I anticipated and greater, I think, than in the Union Army.

We are all human beings and brothers, even though we are carrying on this foolish and tragic war. I treat and try to save the lives of all who are brought to me, for we are all children of God, no matter which side we are on.

God grant that we may soon remember that and make peace with each other. And God grant that you remain well and safe. How often I give thanks that Nell is there in our cabin with you.

Still I sometimes regret that I didn't insist that you should move to a boardinghouse in Asheville, even though I accept your desire to use the knowledge you have acquired over the years to help Nell care for the people of Falling Water Valley during my absence.

And how often I regret that I carried you about from place to place after the death of your dear mother, and left you in the midst of those bitterly disputed mountains, instead of keeping you safely in Washington City. However, we cannot change the past, though I would if I could.

Losing your mother in spite of everything we in the medical profession could do was unbearable to me, but it may have helped to prepare me for the often unsuccessful and always melancholy attempts to save these young boys. They have had their lives destroyed through no fault of their own. Most come from families who have never owned other men or wanted to do other than work their farms for themselves.

In return, the experience of caring for them has forced me, very belatedly, to accept the death of the mother you can barely remember.

Bethany, I ask your forgiveness for the foolish weakness that made me think I could escape my grief by moving again and again to yet another community. Now that you are nearly twenty, you will soon make your own choices about where and with whom you want to spend the rest of your life. But I do promise you that if I sometime get safely back to our home, I want to stop wandering and spend the

rest of my days there in North Carolina's beautiful
Falling Water Valley.

    Forgive my verbosity. Between battles, when I
have time alone, my mind returns to the mistakes I
have made and longs to make them up to you.

    If you can get a letter out to Asheville or
Knoxville, send it in care of the 420th North
Carolina Regiment.

Your loving father,
Ben Andrews

    Bethany Andrews moved her caned chair closer to the candle on the cherrywood table beside her bed and read the letter again, ignoring the chill in the cabin and the cold puncheon floor against her bare feet.

    "At last," she whispered, not taking time to wipe the tears from her brown eyes. "At last. Thank You, God, for whoever brought the letter to my door."

    She read the letter again, not bothering to throw her cape over her coarsely woven nightgown, or stir up the banked fire in the large fireplace at the other end of the room. She was too excited to care about warmth, even after she realized that the letter was nearly three months old.

    She laid the letter on the table and ran her hands through her heavy hair, which hung down nearly to her waist when loose. Then she smiled, recognizing that she was making little progress in breaking herself of that habit that pulled loose strands of brown hair about her face, even when her hair was pinned up.

    "Bethany?" There was a hasty knock on a side door leading to the smaller attached room that was her father's office and bedroom. Before she could respond, the door was opened.

    "Bethany?" Nell Morgan said again. "Something woke me. Did I hear someone running across the porch or did I dream it, since you didn't call me? Is someone sick?"

Bethany ran across the room to throw herself against the angular gray-haired woman. "Oh, Nell, no, it's the greatest news: a letter from Father!"

"In the middle of the night? Are you sure you're not dreaming?"

Bethany laughed. "No, no dream, Nell. See, I'm holding it in my hand." She shook the wrinkled sheets of paper. "I heard a sound at the door and thought someone was coming for help, but when I lit a candle and went to the door, there was no one there. Only this. Someone in the valley brought it to me, then ran."

Nell nodded. "Pretty smart. Carrying letters to Union sympathizers isn't very safe in Falling Water Valley these days. Or to Confederates either, whichever one Ben is called. There's no safety here."

"But come sit down and read it with me." Bethany went to get her candle. She stood beside the table for a few minutes, running her finger across the silken wood grain. It was one of the few things she and her father had carried in their cart when they moved from one place to another in Virginia and North Carolina as he ran from his memories of her mother.

"I'll stir up the fire first. Come over closer." Nell shivered. She had thrown a blanket over her nightgown. Her thinning hair hung over it in wispy strands. "It's cold in here. I'll just heat up the tea left from last night's supper, too."

Bethany moved to one of the leather-laced kitchen chairs that lined the trestle table on the back wall of the cabin near the fireplace. She watched Nell shove their iron kettle deep into the embers to heat, then pour the tea into a silver teapot to celebrate the letter.

"Child," Nell looked at Bethany in the combined light of the candle and blazing fire, "you still haven't put a robe on. You'll catch your death."

She went to the unmade bed at the far end of the room and removed the woolen cape that did double duty as a second blanket. Bethany allowed Nell to slip it around her slim shoulders.

"So where is your father?" Nell asked finally, as she set the teapot and two hand-painted china cups on the unpolished smoothness of the table. Though she probably thought she had controlled her voice to hide the intense personal care she felt for Ben Andrews, Nell's expressive gray eyes gave her away to anyone who knew her as well as Bethany did.

"He didn't say. Just that he is not near here."

"I still can't believe he went with the Rebels. And a lot of people in the Valley just refuse to believe it. They still think he went North. And I'm thinking if he'd known how the bushwhackers would come in and hurt our people, he might have never left at all."

"I know. But he believes that one of God's children is as important as any other. Now stop talking and let me read you the letter," Bethany said, letting her affection for the older woman show in her tone.

She read the letter aloud, unable to get enough of her father's words. Nell listened intently, a slow smile pushing happy wrinkles about her eyes.

Bethany put the letter down and took a sip of the warmed-over sarsaparilla tea. She ran her fingers over the dainty rosebud pattern of her teacup just as she had felt the pattern of the cherrywood table. The table, the teapot, and four china cups that hadn't been broken were all she had of her mother.

Now she was surprised to realize that she had lived in Falling Water Valley longer than any other place since her mother's death. And for one of the five years they had been here, her father had been gone, with she and Nell trying to take his place in the valley.

She smiled lovingly at Nell. When Dr. Andrews had first

struggled with the urgent need for his skills on the battlefield and his reluctance to leave Bethany, Nell had announced that she would stay with Bethany. The day he left, she had appeared at the door carrying a scant armful of clothing.

"It's not proper for a young woman like you to be living alone here," she had announced in her usual pragmatic tone. "I'll just move my herbs and things into Dr. Ben's room 'til he can come home. That way, we'll be closer to each other and better able to work together, too."

Bethany turned from the teacup and picked up the letter again. "Did I tell you that it's nearly three months old? I wonder where it's been all this time."

"Just be glad it finally got here, instead of being lost like the others he wrote," Nell answered. "It's not even midnight yet," she added. "There's still time for a better night's sleep than we get some nights. So let's let the letter be for tonight."

Bethany agreed reluctantly. "I know you haven't been in long from Bertie MacMillan's. Is the baby here?"

"A healthy little girl, yelling like a banshee. She'll make Bertie's misery for losing her husband in this ugly business a little easier. Why Jasper MacMillan went off with the Yankees and got himself killed with the baby coming, I'll never understand. But, that's a man for you, getting all het up over something and thinking crooked about where his responsibilities lie."

As she talked, Nell was carefully pouring the tea from the silver teapot back into the iron one. She drew a gourdful of water from a tin bucket by the fireplace and rinsed the silver one out. Then she expertly banked the fire and went back into her combination office-bedroom. Bethany knew that Nell wouldn't take the time to tend the fire in her own room before she tumbled back into bed.

Bethany still sat at the table. Without conscious direction, her fingers softly stroked her cup again.

She could almost feel again the coolness of her dying mother's cheek as Ben Andrews had held her up to kiss her and hear a whispered, "Good-bye. I love you, little Bethany." Her father's usually firm fingertips were trembling as he tried to be gentle while he wiped away her tears.

Bethany moved her fingers from the cup to her own cheek, as years of memories rushed into her mind. . . .

. . .Looking at the stack of bags and boxes in the back of Daddy's buggy. "Where are we going, Daddy? Are we going to where Mommy is?"

Did he answer her then or the next time they moved, or the next, when the buggy was traded for a cart that could navigate the mountain roads better?

Some of the moves made her happier than others. . . .

. . .In some remote mountain community in Virginia. "Daddy, I like going to school here."

"You'll like the next one, too. Are the children good to you?"

"They like having you here, Daddy. They say you take good care of them."

"That's what I live for now, Bethany. You and being a good doctor every place we go. . ."

. . .Two women overheard somewhere. "Just the same, he's not the only one who ever lost anyone. He ought to settle down and get a mother for that child."

"He's raising her a Christian."

"A Christian should be able to find solace and face up to his loss."

"You know, Widow Brown, Christ told us not to judge. Just because he isn't interested in marrying again. . ."

". . .Daddy, there's a man here who cut his foot."

"Wash it, will you, honey, and get out the dressings. I'll see to it as soon as I finish with this baby. . ."

". . .You've become such a help to me, I don't know what

I'll do if you decide to marry and go off and raise a family. You're my assistant doctor."

"Oh, Daddy, you know I'm not going to marry now. Not for years and years yet."

"But, someday, Bethany. Someday, I'll stop long enough for you to get to know someone well enough to marry. . . ."

Bethany gave the cup a last caress and moved it to the center of the table.

"Whatever forgiveness you think you need, I give you, Daddy," she whispered into the night air. "Every place we were in and every time we moved, I knew you loved me and kept me safe."

He'd stopped in Falling Water Valley long enough for her to get to know the people who lived here and watch the men of the valley leave it for one or the other of the armies. Or to hide out in the surrounding mountains when the conscriptors came into the valley.

The face of Dave Bradley drifted through her mind but she dismissed it. It was time to get back to bed.

She was sure she had barely drifted into sleep when she was wakened by the sounds of gunfire.

two

"Nell, wake up, wake up. People are shooting."

Bethany shook Nell's lank shoulder. She could still hear shooting in the valley over Nell's gentle snores.

"H-m-f-p-t, h-m-f-p-t," Nell muttered, slowly coming out of an exhausted sleep.

"Nell," Bethany repeated, "I know you're tired, but we have to get ready. Someone's raiding the valley."

Nell woke, sat up, and swung her legs over the side of her narrow bed in such an abrupt motion that Bethany jumped back.

"Let's set out the herbs. I've made a lot of lint and I washed the instruments just yesterday." Nell dropped her heavy gown to the floor as she slipped a petticoat and dress over her head, totally indifferent to Bethany's presence. The dress didn't look a great deal different from the gown and petticoat.

She gave her hair a brief run of her fingers, and quickly replaced the pins she'd removed after coming in from helping Bertie MacMillan give birth to her new baby.

Bethany, who had dressed as hurriedly in a loose linsey-woolsey made for her by one of the Valley women, and twisted up her own heavy hair loosely, moved over to the rough wooden cabinet and got down a split elder basket with their precious store of bandages. She placed it on the bare wood top of the long table which they and Dr. Ben used for treatment of those patients who came to the cabin. She put some in her own saddlebags, kept packed with the little medical supplies they had available, and left some for Nell.

She stopped and bowed her head. *God,* she prayed silently, *You know that I'm trying to do a job that's too big for me. Now help me to do good and no harm to everyone. And thank You for Nell.*

Nell came up beside her and allowed her rough hands to caress Bethany's shoulder briefly, but declined Bethany's silent gesture to join hands with her in prayer.

"I prayed while I was dressing, child. In the years I've been working for the people of Falling Water Valley, God and I've come to an understanding that I can't always take time to bow."

Nell had already moved away while she spoke, to dip water from a big bucket in the corner and float a bar of lye soap in it for washing wounds. She shared gentian root, goldenrod, and yarrow infusion with Bethany to be used for cleansing and dressing wounds. She set back their tiny store of turpentine oil to be saved for treatments of infections.

"Nell, I smell smoke. They're burning something."

Nell stopped for a minute, her nose up in the air like a wolf's, as she acknowledged the odor.

"Them's bushwhackers, not regular soldiers," she declared. "There'll be a mighty sight of hurt men and women. Bushwhackers aren't for anyone but themselves no matter what they claim. They just kill and steal for the love of it."

"I don't hear shooting anymore," Bethany said. "They must have moved down the valley."

"We'll be getting wounded in any minute now."

As if she had called the wounded by her comment, they heard a pounding on the door. Bethany went over and lifted the latch.

She opened the door and for a moment, she looked over the head of the woman who stood there, holding a child. A nearby fire threw the blackness of the surrounding mountains into relief against the night sky and played against the bright fall leaves. She could see another fire beyond it.

Smoke drifted a smothering mist against her nostrils. Gunshots sounded farther down the valley, interspersed with howling and barking of dogs.

"They came over the mountain between the Bowers and us and they're just scourgin' their way down the road out."

The sound of Maude MacNeil's voice brought Bethany's attention back to her. "Come in," she said, hearing the fear in her own voice. "Are you hurt?"

As she caught Maude's arm to hurry her inside, she prayed again for strength to help these hurting neighbors of hers feel some measure of security before the night and the day to follow were over. Then she added a silent thanks that the bushwhackers always missed her cabin, which was tucked among the trees just where the hemmed-in valley started to rise toward the surrounding mountains. It gave Nell and her time to get their supplies ready to treat the wounded, and their neighbors a place to go.

"No, Jamie and me heard them coming and run out and hid in the cooling cave, but our haystack is burning. You can see it there. Just set it afire for pure meanness. Now nobody gets the use of it. What'll our cow do now? Maybe if Roy wasn't gone to fight he could have stopped them."

Maude stood holding her child close for a minute, letting tears run uncontrolled down her cheeks. Then the scatter of words began again. "The men will be following them on foot, trying to shoot close enough to make them leave before they fire up the whole valley, but they'll be out too late to do any good. They always are. Raiders know that most all we got left here to fight them is women and old men, so they can plague us anytime they want. I come to help." The last was said more quietly, while she hugged the child to her. "Others'll be here, pretty quick. Them that survive without being hurt."

"Put little Jamie in by the fire in the big room. Make him a pallet back out of the way. We'll need to put people in the floor in there." Nell spoke so calmly that Bethany felt herself growing calmer. She heard another knock at the door.

"That will be Willie with the horses." Bethany tried hard to sound as controlled as Nell, as she picked up the packed saddlebags.

She knew that fifteen-year-old Willie Bowers, who lived with his parents near Bethany and Nell, would have taken Chief and Rainbow out of the stable and back into the trees at the first sounds of a raid. Now that the raiders had moved down the valley, he had brought the horses to take Bethany down to the schoolhouse near the mouth of the valley. If any were wounded in that area they would be brought to her there and other women would come in to help her.

Nell nodded, only taking time to give Bethany a quick hug. "Stay with Willie and be sure the bushwhackers are gone before you go into the schoolhouse," she said. Then in a lower tone, "God go with you."

"I left the horses in the woods, Dr. Bethany," Willie said, as they moved away from the cabin. "Some of the bushwhackers may still be hanging around. We may need to hide."

"I'm not a doctor, Willie," Bethany said automatically. Willie, as well as some of the other Falling Water Valley residents, insisted on giving her the professional title and ignored her protests.

"Let's just hurry," she added, bringing her thoughts back to their journey. It was a couple of miles down to the mouth of the valley where the schoolhouse stood and would be more if they had to dodge into the trees or down one of the lanes which led off the main road down the valley.

She stumbled along behind Willie, wiping tears from her eyes with hands already grimy from smoke and ashes settling from the sky. But she refused to use any of the precious bandages or lint from the saddlebags she carried.

They found the horses standing patiently in their harnesses where Willie had left them. Bethany threw her saddlebags behind the small saddle and mounted her mare, Rainbow, carefully preserving her modesty with her wide skirts, though the young boy seemed to be intent on getting on Nell's big Chief. They guided their horses out to the edge of the trees.

Willie carried an old-fashioned lanthorn, with a large unlit candle inside. He had learned to navigate the valley at night hunting with his father and he used the knowledge now, seeming to know instinctively where downed logs or ditches were. Falling Water Creek was shallow, as usual in autumn, and they forded it easily without needing to use the wooden bridge on the road.

Willie stayed well back from the road and Bethany let him make the decisions. The lights of whatever was burning, that made her able to see most of the time, also made it too dangerous for them to ride in the road. They traveled as fast as they could, sometimes skirting barnyards where animals that had escaped the bushwhackers wandered, sometimes seeing livestock among the trees.

Only at one burning barn did they see any sign of people. A lone woman carried water uselessly, throwing it a bucket at a time on the rapidly burning barn. With a shock, Bethany realized that it was Bertie MacMillan's home place. It would have to be Virgie Smith, who was staying for a few days with Bertie and her newborn baby. She made a move to turn Rainbow toward the barn.

"I'll come back to help her as soon as we get to the school," Willie said in a low tone.

Bethany hesitated, then nodded reluctantly and let Rainbow have her head to follow Chief. By the time Willie got back there would be nothing left of the barn that Virgie was so desperately trying to save. Bethany only prayed that there were no animals inside.

As they moved down the valley, the night became quieter and darker. Down here there were no houses or barns burning, and Bethany considered that the men of the valley had managed to drive the bushwhackers out without further ravages.

From her own knowledge of the valley, she realized that Willie had led her out to the main road and they were coming up on the mouth of the lane which went down to their closed and desolate church.

Bethany never passed this way without feeling tears in her eyes for the closed churches of Falling Water Valley and other communities in the mountains. As always, she breathed a heartfelt prayer for their reopening.

The lane, which had been created by axes and scythes of the first settlers, ancestors of the men and women who until recently had kept it open with their wagons and feet, now was showing neglect. Clumps of tall grasses and the yellow flowers of wild mustard were growing luxuriantly, interspersed with the tragically appropriate ghost flowers, between the wagon paths. But the grass still grew so sparsely where, over the years, wagon wheels and feet had killed its roots, that the paths stood out like straight symbols of hope for a future life for the church.

Bethany felt a hurt within that now when the church was most desperately needed for healing of the bitter conflict between close neighbors and even family members in the mountains, that very strife had caused the minister to flee the valley in fear for his life, and the church doors to be closed. It was a forlorn manifestation of that bigger conflict going on all over the South.

"Dear God," she whispered, "I'm so small and the agony is so big. What can I do to help?"

She had barely finished the prayer when she felt Rainbow shy away from something on the ground at the mouth of the lane.

"Willie," she called softly, "come back. There's something here. I think it's someone. . .hurt."

Willie moved back from his position a few feet in front of her and, seeing the still form on the ground, swung down grabbing both bridles, as Bethany also dismounted.

"Light the candle, Willie."

Reluctantly, Willie opened his lanthorn and used one of his precious stores of lucifer matches. A flicker of light crossed the body of the unfortunate person at their feet.

Though she couldn't see the face, which seemed to have been jammed into a briar patch, the long black-clad legs and huge well-worn leather boots told her that it was a man.

three

She crawled up to the man's shoulders, feeling the trailing blackberry briars snagging her own face and catching on her skirts. A hand on his chest told her that he was still breathing.

"Take his other shoulder and help me pull him out, Willie," she said, since Willie stood without moving.

Willie caught the man's other shoulder and with one impatient gesture, shoved him against Bethany, so that she found herself cradling his upper body and head in her lap. Holding him there, she looked down on his face in dismay.

Scratches from the briars were hardly visible against the bloody, raw flesh of his face. Pieces of skin hung from blackened welts and abrasions. His breath came in puffs from his swollen mouth.

Her whole being went out in sympathy for the unknown man. No one should be beaten like this, no matter who he was. Ignoring Willie's impatience, she gently slipped her hand inside his torn shirt and felt for entry or exit wounds of bullets. He didn't seem to have been shot, though the abrasions and swellings showed further signs of the beating he had taken. Her hands went to his head and found a bleeding knot on the back that probably accounted for his unconscious state.

"Aw, Doctor Bethany, he ain't no one we know. He's nothing but a bushwhacker. Probably my Dad put him there or Uncle Dannel. That's why he's all shoved into the briars."

Bethany agreed that this wasn't a valley man. He could only

be one of the men who had torn through the valley, burning the desperately needed stores that they didn't steal.

She gently laid him back on the ground and wiped the blood off her hand on the grass. She stood up, feeling the same tense pressure to get on to the schoolhouse farther down the valley that Willie was plainly showing. Already, she knew, women were gathering and patients were waiting for her care.

For a minute, she almost felt she could hear her father's words. "I treat all who are brought to me for we are all children of God, no matter which side we're on."

But this was a bushwhacker, a rogue who wasn't on either side, one of those evil men who used the war to excuse their bloody actions.

Still, Bethany heard herself quoting her father. "We are all children of God, Willie."

She made a sudden decision. "Willie, we've got to get him into the church," she said. "He can't get enough good air with all the smoke and ashes out here. And, you know he'll be killed if the men come back and find him."

"Good enough for him," Willie muttered.

"Willie, you're too young to feel that way."

Willie snorted. "I'll be trailin' out to Kentucky to join the Union pretty soon," he said. "Dr. Bethany, let's go. Our own people are at the schoolhouse."

"You know, Willie, he might be Union. All of us look alike and the Yankees raid, too."

"In those clothes? Looks like a slaver to me."

Bethany drew herself up to her full height, almost matching Willie's. She reached into her saddlebag and pulled out a length of heavy cloth that Nell had taught her to use to move patients. She stretched it out to its full length, noticing that it didn't quite come to mid-calf of his long legs.

"Now, help me roll him onto this and we'll get him up to the church and then go on," she said emphatically, hoping she sounded like Willie's commanding mother.

Willie responded. Silently, and letting Bethany know with every grunting step that he disapproved, he walked ahead of her carrying the upper torso of the man while she struggled along between the booted feet, her hands cramping from holding the edges of cloth.

"Be careful not to tramp down any of the grass, Willie. Keep your feet in the wagon tracks," she puffed out as she followed the young boy, feeling like her arms were going to have to let the man go. "Mustn't let anyone know the man is here."

Willie's only answer was a disgusted snort.

Though it was not a long way, Willie sounded as exhausted as she when they finally lowered the body to the low step of the church.

Willie pushed open the unlocked door and, with a grim determined expression that said he was showing her that he was a man grown, picked the stranger off the cloth and carried him into the church.

"Lay him before the front bench, Willie, so if anyone should look in, they won't see him."

Without answering, he carried the man up the aisle and lowered him roughly to the floor in front of one of the two rows of worn, bare-wood benches.

"Can we go now?" he asked, trying to hide his shortness of breath.

Bethany straightened the stranger's head, wishing she could spare a bit of cloth to cushion it, but knowing she would need everything she carried. She rolled her length of cloth and followed Willie out, carefully closing the door behind her.

She had no worry that someone would find him in the unused church, but she wasn't sure about what Willie might do when he saw his father. She turned to him as they walked the short way back to their horses.

"Willie, ordinarily I don't want to encourage you to keep things from your parents, but we need to find out who this man is and why he's here before we tell anyone who might. . . harm him. Can you agree?"

"Dr. Bethany, I ain't a kid. I'm not telling them yet that I'm going to join the North. I can keep this to myself. But, I don't like having that bushwhacker in my Ma's old church."

"A church is a place of haven, Willie. And he doesn't look like he could have done much riding recently. Let's keep an open mind."

Willie gave another barely heard snort as he rode ahead of her again. There was no longer any sound of gunfire, though the smell of smoke and glow of fires behind them still rode on the air, and they could hear a faint sound of shouting from somewhere down below. They took the main road down to the school without talking anymore.

ॐ

Action had already started in the school near the road leading out of the valley when Bethany and Willie arrived. Under the light of several candles and one kerosene lantern set about the small room, Martha Miller and Tabitha Ballard had removed stored blankets from behind the teacher's wooden desk. The sight of the desk brought a momentary sadness that their teacher had closed the school and gone to war.

She pulled her mind back to the present. She could see a large pair of boots sticking out from a bench at the front. Martha was covering a moaning woman who was curled into a shivering ball on a back bench. Recognizing the hysterical woman as the newly delivered mother, Bertie MacMillan, Bethany only took time to quickly wash the stranger's blood off her hands before she sat down beside her.

"Bertie," she said in a low tone, putting both hands on her shoulders, "Bertie, why are you here? Are you hurt? Are you bleeding? Where's the baby?"

Bertie kept her eyes tightly shut and refused to answer. Bethany gently moved her hands over the shaking woman's body while she talked, becoming more puzzled as she found no wounds, and no indication of excessive bleeding from the recent birth.

She looked up at Martha, who had moved to stand beside them. "The man up front," she asked. "Can he wait?"

Martha nodded. "Gunshot," she said in her usual sharp voice, "but he's not bleeding much."

Bethany nodded. "What about Bertie ?" she asked.

"I don't know, Bethany. She just ran in, shaking and crying. We can't get anything out of her."

"Bertie," Bethany spoke more urgently as Martha moved back toward the front of the school, "you've got to talk to me. Where is the baby? You must tell me, Bertie."

Bertie drew in a shuddering breath, and looked intently at Bethany, seeming to recognize her for the first time. "She's gone, Bethany," she spoke between sobs in a shaky voice. "I don't know. . ."

Bethany slid to her knees, praying almost without words, as she gathered Bertie into her arms. "Tell me. Tell me, Bertie."

"Oh, Bethany, Virgie Smith was staying with me and Baby since. . .we're alone in the world. When we heard the ruckus, she built up the fire in the fireplace, and. . .ran home to her kids, because she knew her man would. . .chase the raiders. . ." Bertie's voice was trembling, her words coming slowly, as though she was forcing them out.

"At first, I thought it was the fireplace. . .that was making it so light inside. Then I saw. . .it was the barn on fire." She stopped as though she had forgotten what she was trying to tell.

Bethany stroked Bertie's back, and she felt a slight easing of the tremor in the body she held. She forced her hand to move slowly on Bertie's back, even as she felt tension building inside herself, as another man limped in and sat down on a bench. Tabitha threw a blanket over his shoulders.

Bethany tried not to take her gaze from Bertie's face as words seemed to come more easily to continue her story.

"I carried Baby outside with me in case one of the raiders might come inside and find her. . .you know? I went in the barn for old Bess. We can't afford to lose her. I need milk to drink to keep me feeding Baby."

Again she seemed to forget what she was telling. *God, help me to be patient,* Bethany prayed silently. A quick glance showed her that Tabitha Ballard was washing a gash on the leg of the last man brought in.

Bertie drew a deep breath and went on. "Old Bess wasn't in there. I guess the raiders took her. But I thought I could save the barn. I put Baby down on a soft pile of leaves while I drew water to throw on the barn."

Bethany felt a shudder go through her own body as she realized it was Bertie they had passed before they stopped to help the stranger. What if one of their horses had stepped on the baby? But they hadn't passed that close, she remembered with relief.

"The fire was ahead of me. I couldn't stop it and I gave up and went to get Baby. . ." Suddenly Bertie screamed. The howling sound reverberated through the tiny schoolhouse. Martha and Tabitha stopped their work and jerked around to stare.

"She's gone. Baby's gone," Bertie screamed, sitting bolt upright and clutching Bethany with frantic hands. "When I went to pick Baby up, she was gone. Some wild animal took her. . .or some raider. I ran down here to get someone to help me hunt for her."

Bethany felt someone beside her and looked up to see Willie. "Dr. Bethany," he said, "I was going back to help fight the fire.

I'll take Bertie back and find the baby. We can ride double on Chief." He sounded like the man he wanted Bethany to see in him. Then he fell back into being a little boy as he said, "I might have been back in time to help her if we hadn't stopped." His expression told Bethany what he thought of taking precious time to help one of the enemy.

"I know, Willie. But we can only take care of what God puts in front of us. We can't know. . ." Bethany let the thought drift off. She turned back to Bertie.

"Bertie, Willie is going to take you back to look for the baby. You must stand up and go show him where you put Baby down. For Baby's sake. Do you understand?"

Bertie nodded dumbly. Bethany and Willie helped the distraught woman to stand. After a few minutes, Bertie walked out unsteadily with Willie. Bethany noticed with satisfaction that Willie carefully supported her as they went out. Willie was going to make a fine man.

Sending a prayer after the two, and seeing that Tabitha seemed to have the wounded leg cleansed and bandaged, she walked up the aisle to the big boots she had seen earlier. They didn't seem to have moved, and she wondered if the man wearing them was unconscious.

She walked around the bench and looked down at the man. He was lying with his eyes closed. His face was pale but he didn't seem to be in pain. Seeming to feel her presence, he opened brown eyes and, with an evident effort, forced his usual jovial expression onto his long face.

"Bethany, I've been waiting for you."

"Dave. Martha didn't tell me it was you."

He grinned. "I know. She said you were busy with Bertie." He grunted. "Lost her baby. That Bertie MacMillan always was a dizzy one."

"Dave Bradley." Bethany looked at him seriously. "Can you imagine how a parent feels when a child is missing?"

He winked at her. "No, but I will when we get hitched and have a whole passel of kids."

Bethany didn't respond to his teasing mood. Dave Bradley had been half-seriously courting her for about a year, but she wasn't at all sure that he was the man she wanted to marry. He never seemed to be serious about anything. But he always hurried out to help chase the raiders out of the valley.

She could see him wince with pain when he moved his leg, even though he tried to hide it. Immediately, she became the attendant, there to help.

"Dave, where is it? The bullet?"

"In my left leg. Inside my boot."

He turned his leg inward and she could see a small hole in his knee-high boot. He groaned, then tried to cover it with a joke. "Shucks! And I bought those boots in Ashville back before the war. Never find another pair now."

Bethany gently picked up the leg. "I've got to pull the boot off, Dave. It's going to hurt. Want me to cut it off instead?"

Dave looked undecided, then his vanity got the best of him. "No! I'll not lose the boot completely. Pull it off."

"For shame, Dave Bradley, asking a young girl like Bethany to pull off your boot. Just don't you go thinking that because she's a medical person, you don't have to respect her. Bethany, I'll pull that boot off." Martha Miller appeared at Bethany's elbow, using a pointing forefinger to make her disapproval more evident.

But, in the end, it took both of them to get the boot off, Martha holding onto his leg and Bethany pulling at the boot, while Dave gritted his teeth. As the boot finally came off in Bethany's hand, the bullet dropped to the floor with a dull thud.

"It's just a scratch," Martha said sharply, though a painful gouge showed in Dave's calf. "I'll take care of this one. You don't need to bother."

Bethany knew that the older woman was considering herself a keeper of what was proper between the two young people. Since the wound didn't seem to be bleeding much, Bethany let Martha take care of it, and left her washing it out well and preparing to apply a dressing dampened with a solution of gentian.

This raid seemed to have produced a smaller than usual number of injuries. Bethany cleansed and dressed a few wounds then told Tabitha and Martha she was leaving.

She had two things in mind. To see if Bertie and Willie had found the baby and to check on the stranger they had left in the church.

four

Bethany had hardly noticed the dulling of the candles as daylight crept into the school, but it struck her tired eyes with full force as she stepped outside.

A gentle mist curling up the sides of the mountains which enclosed the valley had replaced the smoke of the night before. The rim of the sun was just sending flashes of light down through it from the east. The late October morning was chilly, but she knew it would soon warm up under that sun.

For a moment, Bethany just stood and looked about her with the intense pleasure that overtook her at every sunrise and sunset. She whispered her usual morning prayer, a simple "Thank You" to God for the coming day and the mountain beauty that surrounded them.

Rainbow, still wearing her saddle, grazed contentedly on the drying grass. She whinnied gently on seeing Bethany and came to her. Bethany rubbed her nose and ears then replaced the bridle that Willie had taken off and mounted her.

Duty to the valley people and worry about the baby took her to the home of Bertie MacMillan first. As she passed the mouth of the lane leading down to the church where they had left the stranger, she looked intently at the little bit she could see of the church.

Though she couldn't tell if the door was closed, she could see no sign in the now full daylight that the stranger had awakened and come out. Hurrying so that she could come back and see about him, Bethany urged her horse on.

At the two-room MacMillan home, she found that Nell had

visited and had given a potion to Bertie, who was well into a sleep of exhaustion.

"Nell, have they found the baby?" she whispered.

Nell shook her head grimly. With a twinge, Bethany realized how tired Nell looked after a night of almost no sleep. It seemed like days instead of hours since they had read Ben Andrews' letter together.

Nell led Bethany out into the morning air. They stood at the back of the cabin overlooking the ashes where the barn had stood. The background of brightly leafed trees on a gentle rise seemed already to be taking the place of the missing barn. The faint odor of burning wood still disturbed their nostrils.

"Old Bess came back to be milked early this morning, but Baby. . .there's no sign. The men, those who weren't hurt last night, and some that were, are out looking, but, Bethany, I'm afraid. A baby that young can't live long without its mother, even if it was a human and not an animal that took it."

Bethany looked at her intently, as the new thought she'd brought up penetrated her mind.

"Are you thinking somebody took the baby? But, who?"

"It's hard to imagine why the bushwhackers might want to take a baby, but they're evil, Bethany. They're just evil. Maybe just to kill it."

Bethany thought of the stranger she and Willie had left in the church. He couldn't possibly have had anything to do with Baby's disappearance, but with the passion in the valley growing greater with this tragedy, some of the men would take their anger and frustration out on him.

She and Willie must never let anyone know that he was there.

She gave Rainbow to Nell to ride back to their cabin, not wanting her to trample the high grass and weeds on the lane to the church and show that someone had been there. She told Nell truthfully that she was going back to see about a patient, which gave her a reason to carry the saddlebags with her. She hurried off toward the empty church where she and Willie had left the stranger, becoming more anxious with every step.

She stood on the flat stone step for a few minutes, waiting for her heartbeat to slow down. Her gaze went to the cemetery. Though the grass and weeds had been pulled off one or two of the individual graves, they had mostly been allowed to grow high just as they had in the lane and surrounding the church. Did the anger and ill will growing daily in the valley community make them not want to care for the cemetery which held the ancestors of them all?

Surely that was something she could convince the warring neighbors to tend. They couldn't lose the respect for their forebears who had braved so many obstacles to make Falling Water Valley the place it used to be.

Slowly, then, she opened the handleless door, pushing it inward. She hurried down the aisle to the front bench. The stranger laid where she and Willie had left him. Was he dead? Breathless, she knelt beside him.

A hand on his chest told her that he was breathing. Bethany wished for her father's hollow listening tube that was back at the cabin. She laid her ear to his chest. Both his breathing and heartbeats were coming with regularity and she heard no muffled sounds of congestion. She straightened and prepared to examine the bruises and abrasions about his head.

❧

The man felt a pressure on his chest that caused a soft pain as that of rubbing a sore spot on a foot. For a moment he was aware of more pain in his face and body. Feeling, for a reason he didn't know how to analyze, that he mustn't allow himself to groan, he carefully opened his eyes as the pressure on his chest suddenly eased.

A confused picture of a woman's face surrounded by brown hair softly billowing in slow waves into and out of surrounding light was too much for his wandering mind. Was she an. . .he couldn't think of the word that seemed to hover in the background of his mind.

He let his eyes drift shut and his mind drift back into nothingness.

৵

Did his eyes open? Kneeling above him, Bethany wasn't sure. Maybe it was just an illusion of movement that she could have imagined. But it would be easier for him if she treated his wounds while he was still unconscious. Opening her saddlebag, she took out several pledgets of linen soaked in yarrow solution and proceeded to gently cleanse the bruises and cuts on his face, noting thankfully that none of the cuts were deep enough to need her father's sewing needle.

Leaving them open to the air, she proceeded to the swelling on the back of his head. She turned his head and again felt a tiny movement under her hand. She hurried to care for that wound.

It was swollen and ugly. Most of the blood on the floor had come from it. She remembered her father's admonition that scalp wounds did swell and bleed copiously and were best left open to heal. A scar on the back of the head was of no consequence and the wound did better if it drained.

She cleansed the wound as best she could, wishing she had brought some of Nell's soap to wash the dried blood from the dark hair which hung in soft waves over the rest of his head, touching his collar in the back. Feeling the underlying softness under her hands as she worked on the wound, she wondered how it could be so well cared for in the wild, uncouth life of a bushwhacker. Still, some of them lived at home somewhere over the mountains when they weren't raiding.

Abruptly, she brought her mind back from wondering about his life. He was just a stranger who had undoubtedly done much harm to the people of the valley and would just as undoubtedly be harmed by the men of the valley if they knew he was there. The fact that he was an exceedingly handsome stranger wasn't important.

She felt a momentary guilty disloyalty to the valley people for hiding and caring for an enemy until she remembered her father's words, "We are all children of God. . ." She couldn't just walk away from one of God's children.

She had done all she could for his face and head and turned her attention to his muscular chest. A careful examination through the tatters of shirt left on him showed numerous bruises, one on the left so discolored that she thought a rib might be broken. She determined not to try to turn him until she could bring back a length of cloth to brace the chest.

A swift check of his long legs let her know that they seemed to move easily and she didn't see any deep gashes through the tears in the heavy material of the pants which were tucked into knee-high boots. She didn't attempt to examine them further. Perhaps Willie could give them a closer inspection for her.

Remembering the possibility that his eyes had opened for a second, she determined to come back at the end of the day and attempt to get some fluid into him. She covered him well with the blanket. This time she placed his head on a folded piece of torn blanket. Then, picking up her saddlebags, she carefully looked out the one glassed window to be sure that no one was about before venturing outside.

Walking up the incline of the valley to Bertie's house, Bethany realized how tired she was. The nearly empty saddlebags seemed too heavy to lift and her legs shook as she went to the door of the cabin. The scene inside didn't help her.

Bertie lay in a deep sleep on the old-fashioned pole bed attached to a hole in the log wall. Tabitha Ballard had come up from the school to relieve Virgie Smith. She stood by the fireplace with an expression of worry that told Bethany the baby hadn't been found.

She thought of the bushwhacker she had just treated. He might have been the one who fired the barn before the valley men had come on him and taken their anger at the cruel raids out on him. Yet if the valley people had beaten him and left him for dead, why hadn't she heard someone talking about it? The men wouldn't hesitate to gloat over getting revenge on one of the bushwhackers.

Her tired mind refused to consider anything more. She only wanted to forget this night and lie down and sleep for a long time. Yet she couldn't go off and leave this sad house.

Tabitha seemed to read her distress. "No need to walk up to your cabin, Bethany, and there's nothing you can do here. Just stretch out beside Bertie. I'll watch and wake you if they. . . find Baby."

"What of your own sleep, Tabitha? And what of the men in the schoolhouse?"

"They've all gone home. Except for her and her baby," she jerked her head toward the sleeping Bertie, "we were lucky this time. A couple of barns burned, a few pigs gone, not many hurt. But the men are savage about the baby. Any bushwhackers still around, they'd better skedaddle."

God, how can I feel this guilt for helping a human? Bethany barely remembered the need to find Willie and remind him to keep their secret, before her tired body relaxed on the cornhusk mattress beside Bertie and she sank into a deep sleep.

੨੦

In the church, the man opened his eyes again, with a vague memory of something, two faces above him. . .faces very different from each other. . .hair of different colors. . .again he couldn't think of a word for either one. . .or any reason for being here. . .or any place he might have been before. He had a nagging need to remember something but, like waking from a dream that drifts away, he found nothing to remember.

Moving was painful. Just being awake was painful and, wherever he was, he seemed to be alone. He let himself drift back into the vacuum.

❧

Bethany woke to the sound of angry voices and loud weeping. Without raising up, she looked around. Bertie was huddled in a blanket by the fireplace, Tabitha standing beside her. They both stared out the open door where several men with rifles milled around. A huge carcass of a black bear stretched out by the door, its head on the step.

"Oh, no!" Bethany jerked herself upright. "Tabitha, is it. . . ? Did the bear. . . ?"

Tabitha turned from Bertie's side, her hands still on her shoulders. "We didn't find Baby yet. The men took their mad out on the bear. It's been a bad night and day here. There's a note for you."

Standing up and unfolding the piece of smudged paper, Bethany realized that it was Willie's mother who was standing to the side of the fireplace facing away from the room and crying. Bertie was staring silently, almost in a daze.

Even before she read the note, Bethany guessed what it would say. "I'm going, Dr. Bethany. I didn't tell."

Bethany bowed her head. *God, am I wrong to try to save the stranger's life? Have I sent Willie off to lose his? Please keep Willie safe.*

She became aware that Tabitha still stood beside her. "Bethany Andrews, how long has it been since you ate anything?"

Bethany smiled ruefully. "I don't believe I remember, Tabitha. I need to go up and see if Nell needs help. I shouldn't have let myself sleep."

"Now, Nell can wait until you've had yourself a good meal. Maybe you can get Bertie to eat a bite, too. I haven't been able to. Haven't been able to get Annie Bowers to act like a woman grown about her son going to war like all our sons and husbands, either."

While Bethany pulled a chair up beside Bertie and placed an arm about her shoulders, Tabitha dipped up fragrant bowls of vegetable soup from a huge vat she was keeping hot in the ashes of the fireplace. She handed them both to Bethany and dropped a round corn pone in the edge of each.

"After the men get the bear butchered, I'll boil some up and put it in the soup. Nothing more nourishing than bear meat."

Bethany put her own bowl down while she talked gently to Bertie, trying to bring her back to her responsibility to the missing baby. "I know it hurts, Bertie, but you must eat so that you can nurse Baby when the men find her."

Bertie didn't straighten her drooping shoulders or take the bowl from Bethany's hand, but like a child herself, she opened her mouth and let Bethany spoon the nourishing soup into it.

Before Bethany had emptied the bowl, Bertie turned her head away. "Bethany, I didn't even name her. Just called her Baby. How is Jasper and my mother going to know who she is in heaven if she doesn't even have a name?"

Bethany put the bowl down on the hearth and gathered Bertie's shrunken shoulders into her arms. "Bertie, God takes care of us in heaven and we've been told we will know our own. But He takes care of us here, too. Baby is in His hands wherever she is. And He knows her name."

She felt Bertie's body make a small movement toward her own and relax a bit.

"I was thinking of calling her Sally after my mother," she whispered.

"Sally. That's a lovely name," Bethany said. "Shall we start calling her Sally now?"

Bertie nodded. "It was just that after Jasper was killed, I. . . almost stopped believing that God cared. . .and with the church closed and all. . .and no preacher to talk to. . .and now

Baby. . .Sally. . .Bethany. . .where's the church?"

Bethany shook her head. "I don't know, Bertie." She felt remorse that she couldn't say anything else. Surely there was some way they could get the differing people of the valley to come together and accept the comfort of the church again.

She sighed, then stood up. There was no more she could do here. She needed to go home and see if Nell needed help. After a few words with Annie who had reduced her sobs to sniffles, she left the cabin, carefully walking around the carcass of the bear.

Dave Bradley wasn't with the men butchering the bear. He must be lying down in his own house built a little way up the side of the mountain. That leg wound was small but it would be painful.

Willie's father was there, grimly chopping at the meat as though to let out the anger inside himself. So was Bertie's father-in-law, but Carl Dietz, whose only son had been killed by a Union bullet wasn't. Bethany wasn't surprised. Carl Dietz was too bitter to come out for even a baby belonging to Northern sympathizers.

She tried to not look at the magnificent body of the bear now being turned into quivering chunks of meat by the angry men. But she hesitated for a moment, listening for some mention of the man she'd found unconscious down by the church. She heard none.

five

Nell was alone at the cabin table, drinking a cup of herbal tea. Though Bethany was sure she hadn't slept since they had been awakened the night before, her eyes were bright and sharp as she greeted her and motioned to a chair at the table. Bethany poured herself a cup of tea and sat down.

"Well, as raids go, that one wasn't too bad. No one bad hurt," Nell said.

Bethany nodded. She was afraid to give a report on her own night's activities. The observant woman across the table from her was too apt to guess that she was leaving something out. She only told her that she had slept at Bertie's and that the men had killed a bear.

"What can be done about Bertie's baby?"

Nell snorted. "Bertie ought to be horsewhipped for leaving that baby on a pile of leaves. Like as not some catamount's carried it off. The raiders had already gone by. One thing, these raids and now the baby gone get the people to work together for a little while, even if they don't stop hating each other. Anybody gone to ask old Mountaintop Mattie how to find her?"

"Nell, she's not a godly woman."

Nell took a long drink from her cup. "True, she's not a godly woman, but some people believe she's able to find things with her second sight. . .I think that she knows where things are because she stole them and put them there."

"Do you think she may have taken Baby?"

"I don't know. It wouldn't be unchristian to go up and find out. She's a strange old woman and she's watching us more than we know about when she decides to come down off that mountain. And she's got hiding places up there that we don't know about, too."

Bethany looked thoughtful. "If we're going up to see if she has Baby, I agree that it would be a Christian thing to do. But you're much too tired to go up there and, anyway, somebody needs to be here in case they find another wounded person. I'll go."

To her surprise Nell didn't object. "I'm not afraid that Mattie can put anything over on you with her pretense of special powers. And I have to admit a nap would be good."

Rainbow was grazing desultorily beside the stable. She submitted to the bridle and saddle and trotted easily a short way down the valley to the widest trail up the mountain. Though Bethany was going up on a serious errand, rather than the rides she sometimes took for sheer pleasure, she couldn't help responding to the splendor of fall colors of yellows and reds against the mix of evergreens as Rainbow carried her up the mountainside.

Rainbow stopped on her own on a large overhanging rock where she often carried Bethany to look down on the valley, reveling in the beauty, and praying for the safety of her father as well as other men of the valley who were off fighting on both sides of the war. Bethany sometimes dismounted and sat on the rock watching the grace of lowly buzzards almost seeming to play as they drifted about the sky, soaring on the winds in the valley. Even God's scavengers appeared to enjoy His world, maybe more than some people did.

She found herself looking for the birds today to see if they might be circling over a small body on the mountainside. She shuddered at the thought and sighed with relief that she saw only a lone raven flying against the afternoon sun.

"We're not stopping today, Rainbow," she said aloud, urging her on. She scolded herself for allowing the fables about ravens to cause a feeling of fear. After all, ravens were God's creatures, too.

She concentrated on the knock-knocking of a big woodpecker back in the woods, and was grateful for the quick glimpse of the majestic multicolors of a tom turkey moving away from her to the side of the trail. Then she pushed Rainbow to go a little faster. Sunlight was slanting too low through the trees for her comfort.

Mattie lived in a tumbledown, one-room shack, nestled against a rock outcropping. According to what Bethany had heard, she had built the cabin herself, from logs she had filched from houses being built in the valley below. To Bethany's eyes, the huge woman looked quite capable of cutting and dressing the mismatched logs herself.

She sat in the open doorway with her moccasined feet perched on the edge of a flat rock, which served as a front step. She wore a tanned deerskin around her shoulders over a loosely fitting and mismatched blouse and skirt.

She didn't move as Bethany rode Rainbow out into the clearing around the cabin, but her eyes followed them.

"I saw you coming," she called. "I saw you when you left your cabin." She shoved the deerskin a bit off her shoulders and straightened her back. Bethany forced herself not to think of a prehistoric queen on a stone throne. She was so big. Even sitting down, Mattie looked both tall and heavy.

Bethany turned and looked at the tree-covered mountain behind her. It was impossible for anyone to see her cabin, and she decided not to give Mattie the satisfaction of pointing that out to her. Mattie would only insist that she used her "second sight" to see her.

She slipped off Rainbow and let the reins drag on the ground, knowing that the mare had learned to stay near while she performed services for some sick person. Rainbow placidly started grazing the wild grasses in the clearing.

Bethany forced herself not to show any emotion as she moved toward the impassive figure in the doorway. Somehow she must get Mattie to let her into the cabin so she could see if Baby Sally was in there.

"I know why you came. And you're not the first to come up here today to ask me to deevine the whereabouts of that mean Bertie's baby. She didn't treat that baby right, leaving it on a pile of leaves."

Bethany remembered that Nell had said the same thing and probably everyone in the valley agreed with her. But she remained silent, waiting for Mattie to continue.

"Well, I told them that there's someone that they don't know is in Falling Water Valley. Maybe took the baby to do it harm. A stranger."

Mattie lifted her eyelids slightly and gave Bethany a look of pure evil out of shiny blue eyes. Bethany forced herself not to shudder and to return look for look. Mattie's theatrics were silly, and she determined not to give her the satisfaction of reacting.

"I haven't come to ask you to divine anything," she said firmly. "You know I don't believe your pretense of special powers. I've come to ask you if you've seen the baby." She deliberately emphasized the word "seen".

Mattie chuckled and pulled back full lips to show surprisingly white teeth. She pulled a broken comb out of the depths of the mismatched pieces of clothing she wore and ran it through the dirty gray hair which hung loosely down her back to her waist.

"I've only seen her with my third eye," she announced dramatically, shoving her arms, the comb still in her hand, out toward the mountainside.

"Stop the silly acting," Bethany repeated firmly. "You

know I don't accept such nonsense."

"Oh, you don't," Mattie said. She raised her eyelids till they seemed to disappear inside her head. "Then maybe you might be surprised to hear that I know where the stranger in the valley is. The one someone is hiding from her righteous neighbors in their own church."

Bethany gasped before she could catch herself. Then she looked full into Mattie's eyes. "So you were down in the valley during the raid. Will you let me search your cabin for Baby?"

For a moment, Mattie showed her surprise that her dramatics hadn't achieved the awe they usually did. Then the lids dropped over her eyes again. She seemed to hesitate before she pushed herself upright with her hands. Bethany thought she recognized a surprising look of intense pain as she rose to her full height. But Mattie controlled it and stepped away from the door.

"Come on in, lessen you're afraid," she said with her full-lipped smile.

Bethany did feel a little discomfort at the thought of going with the huge woman into the small dim room she could see through the doorway. But there was no other way she could see if Baby Sally was in there. She took a deep breath, pretending not to notice Mattie's widening smile at her discomfort, and followed the woman inside. She noticed that Mattie walked with a strong limp, as though putting weight on her right leg may have caused the pain Bethany had noted before.

It was like walking into a cave. The huge rock that Mattie had built on served as a floor. Another rock was the back wall. There was a dampness in the hut that Bethany suspected never went away, even in summertime.

As her eyes adjusted to the dimness, Bethany saw that a blackened area covered with ashes showed that Mattie simply built a campfire on the rock floor to cook or heat with. A piece of board propped on flat rocks against one side of the hut served as a shelf. There was little on it except a blackened iron spider-legged skillet.

A pile of tanned furs were stacked against the huge rock that reared up higher than the roof of the cabin. They looked like a fairly comfortable bed, but there was no baby in it.

There was nothing in the cabin to show that Mattie had the baby or that she could have fed it if she did.

"See anything?" Mattie asked. "And what do you think will happen when the valley people find out about the man in the church?"

There was a definite threat in her voice. She raised her eyelids sharply again. Her eyes almost seemed to sparkle from some light not present in the dim cabin.

"For some salve for my sore leg, I'll deevine who the stranger is for you." Her eyes threw out a challenge.

Bethany refused to take up the challenge. "I have no belief in your ability to divine anything," she repeated for the third time. "But I will try to treat your leg. Will you show it to me?"

Mattie, seeing that her repeated attempts at dramatics weren't making any impression on Bethany, turned and walked out of the cabin without answering. Bethany thought she was making a strong effort not to limp. She followed her out.

"I don't take something for nothing. For not talking about the man you're hiding, then," Mattie said, her voice showing that she had given up her pretense of being all-knowing.

Bethany walked away from the cabin and caught up the mare's reins, mounting easily. She enjoyed the sensation of looking down on Mattie.

"Do whatever you want to, Mattie," she said. "Whatever you choose to do, if you'll come down to our home, Nell and I will treat your leg."

Mattie frowned, a frown that seemed to cover her whole face. She turned away without answering and strode off into the trees in an opposite direction from the trail down the mountain that Bethany would take.

Bethany fought down a desire to go to the church to check on the stranger before she went home. It was getting dark and she needed to talk to Nell.

She was relieved to find Nell sitting at the table when she walked into the big room of the cabin after unharnessing Rainbow and putting her in the stable.

"Nell, you don't look like you've moved. Did you take a nap?"

Nell smiled. "Sometimes a fifteen-minute nap can do as well as several hours. There's some sarsaparilla in the kettle, and hot hoecake on the hearth. Sit down and tell me about Mattie."

Bethany poured herself a cup of tea, added a dollop of honey to it and smeared some of the honey on the hot hoecake. Not trying to hide her troubled expression, she sat across from Nell.

She told her what had happened on the mountain, leaving out Mattie's knowledge of the stranger in the church. "I don't see any way she can have the baby," she added.

"She'll do to keep an eye on, anyway," Nell answered. "She knows that mountain like the back of her hand. There's a lot of places up there she can hide what she doesn't want found. But why she'd want to. . ." Nell spread her hands in a gesture of bewilderment. "Surely she knows that we'll treat her leg, whatever the problem is, for the asking. We don't turn anyone away."

Bethany remembered Mattie's strong need to give something in return for anything done for her. A need that took the form of a threat now.

She took a soothing mouthful of tea and swallowed it slowly. Without tasting the bread, she set the cup on the table with sudden decision.

"Nell, I need to tell you something."

six

Nell smiled affectionately. "I thought you might." She sat back, letting her hands fall into her lap, and giving her full attention as Bethany explained about the man at the church.

"Of course you did the right thing, Bethany. Your father's daughter couldn't do anything but care for anyone who needs it."

For a moment Nell let her gaze drift away and Bethany knew that she was thinking of Ben Andrews. Bethany believed that the older woman sheltered stronger feelings toward her father than she admitted to.

Nell stood up with determination. "We'll go down to check on him in the morning before it gets light enough for people to see us. Now we'll sleep."

Bethany was sure that Nell, used to accepting sleep whenever she could get it, fell into slumber immediately. But, tired as she was, she felt recent events playing themselves over and over in her mind before she finally drifted off.

❧

Down in the church, the man floated to some dim surface of consciousness, filled with pain and a confused sense of a light in the darkness and someone moving above him. He opened his eyes. A huge face with a jack-o'-lantern white-toothed grin, surrounded by floating gray hair was almost against his. Frightened, he tried to push himself up.

The face disappeared and he heard a door slam somewhere.

❧

Bethany woke to Nell's brisk shaking of her shoulder. A candle stood on the table, telling her that it must be still dark.

"Hurry, Bethany," Nell admonished. "I slept too long. It's going to be daylight before we get down to the church as it is."

Quickly Bethany got up, dressed, and followed Nell into the side room. "Maybe it's just as well, Nell. A light in the church might be noticed more than us going down the valley to take care of someone."

Nell nodded briskly, beginning to refill the saddlebags from various containers set on a shelf above the table. Neither mentioned breakfast.

"Let's just take one horse." Bethany spoke while filling a jug with soup from the kettle that simmered on the hearth. She got down a bowl and a tin spoon from the shelf above the table. Maybe the stranger might be awake enough that she could get some liquids into him without choking him. She remembered her father's admonitions of the importance of keeping fluids in the body.

Nell agreed impatiently. "We'll ride Chief double so both horses won't be outside the church. We'll go in the back of the church so he doesn't leave a trail down the lane. Let's get going. That man may need more care now."

Nell harnessed Chief, so adept at throwing on bridle and saddle that she didn't need light. Bethany favored walking but Nell insisted that would slow them down too much. She threw the saddlebags over her own shoulder. Bethany, stepping on their mounting stump lifted herself up to sit sidewise behind Nell, clinging uncomfortably to the back of the saddle.

≈

"He's been unconscious for a full day now. That isn't a good sign, is it, Nell?"

"Maybe. Maybe not. With head injuries it's hard to tell." Nell pushed the church door open, impatiently. Bethany almost laughed. Nell was always like that when she wanted to get to someone who needed her.

They walked carefully down the aisle to the front bench then stopped abruptly. In the pale light of early morning the stranger was leaning on his right elbow, dark brown eyes wide with apprehension, a muscular arm held out as though to ward off more blows. He had kicked off the blanket Bethany had left on him, and his long legs in their boots were drawn up as though ready to defend himself.

Bethany stepped back against the pulpit, letting Nell go forward toward the bushwhacker.

"Well," Nell said briskly, going down on her knees beside him. "So you're awake. Just lay back now. We're not going to hurt you. Though we are going to send you on your way as soon as we can. If the local men who caught you and beat you up realize that Bethany's been hiding you, they'll finish the job they started."

All the time she was talking, Nell was giving the man a thorough going-over. Bethany recognized her method of random talk to keep her patients' attention while she examined or treated them. Many patients found it comforting.

Bethany moved closer, ready to help, but Nell shook her head. "Looks like he's just going to be a bit sore. I don't see any broken bones. Can't tell about that rib, but he's breathing easy so it can't be poking into his lung. Just let me get this cloth strapped around him."

The stranger cooperated with her while she slipped a long piece of cloth under his shirt and tied it in front, grimacing with pain when she had him turn. "Now," she looked the man full in the eyes, "just for the record, tell us who you are and why someone who looks as smart as you was riding with the bushwhackers."

The man looked puzzled. He seemed to be considering whether he should talk or not. After several minutes he shook his head.

"I don't. . .know."

"Come on, man. You don't think I'm daft, do you?"

He looked from one to the other of the women with an expression that was half-puzzled, half-frightened, then shook his head again, saying nothing.

"Nell, maybe he's telling the truth. He's had a really bad blow on the head."

Nell sat back on her heels. She looked at the man contemplatively for a long period. He met her gaze without any change in his puzzled expression.

"Maybe you are," Nell said. "Maybe you aren't. But, either way, we'll watch you here for awhile, then try to get you out of the valley without anyone knowing."

"Why?"

Bethany almost jumped. He must be telling the truth that he didn't remember or else he was a great actor.

"Just what do you remember? And keep in mind that we know you were with the bushwhackers," Nell said.

He only shook his head again, not answering.

"Nell, let me get some food into him before he tires out," Bethany whispered.

Nell stood up and Bethany took her place. Kneeling, she poured a small amount of soup into a bowl and slowly brought a spoonful to his mouth.

He swallowed the soup gratefully, tasting a sensation that brought a short-lived feeling of familiarity into the blank grayness that was his mind. After a few swallows, he let his gaze wander away from the lovely face that had replaced the older one above him.

From where he lay, he could see only the rough boards that made up benches that seemed to be around him. The woman in front of him was a much more inviting view and he returned his gaze to her. Why did she and the other keep insisting that he should leave? And that he knew a name he should tell them? A faint sense of syllables drifted through his mind. Too faint and too fast for him to hold them. He closed his eyes.

"He's tired. Sleeping'll be best for him now." Nell reached down for the bowl. "He just needs to let nature heal his bruises."

"Isn't there some way we can make him more comfortable, Nell? He's been lying on the floor for so long now."

"A lot of wounded soldiers are lying on hard floors, or out in the weather, all over the South," Nell answered, without much sympathy. "He should be thankful just to be inside. And remember, Bethany, why he's here."

"I don't know why, but I can't believe he's one of them," Bethany answered. She looked over at the little cast-iron stove, where no fire had been lit for such a long time. "I. . .It probably wouldn't be safe to build a fire in case it turns cold before we get back."

Nell looked at her in surprise. "Are you daft, child? Smoke coming out of the church chimney when no one's been in here in months?"

Bethany felt herself flush as she nodded her agreement with Nell's common sense. Was she somehow losing her own in her desire to help the man resting on the floor and now seeming to drift away from them again?

&

Floating off to sleep, the man let their words wander through his mind. Why was he here and why did they seem to think he had done something bad? Why did they think he was in danger? And why were their words the only thing in his mind? Again those meaningless syllables crossed his mind too rapidly to catch, and he returned gratefully to that more total blankness where there were no mysterious questions.

&

Bethany followed Nell out reluctantly. "I think I'll walk back," she said. "Chief will appreciate that."

Nell looked at her for a long moment. Then she nodded her head. "But, don't think we won't need to talk about getting this man out of the valley."

They went into the stand of trees behind the church where Nell had tied Chief loosely to be sure he didn't wander out in front of the church. He stood patiently while she fastened the familiar saddlebags behind his saddle then easily lifted herself to his back. Without looking again at Bethany, she yanked on his bridle and guided him out into the trees to come out onto the road farther up the valley.

Bethany walked across to the cemetery, feeling the wet grass and weeds dragging against her long skirt. She grieved again for the time when the men of the valley came in regularly with their scythes to keep the churchyard cut clean.

It was as though both church attendance and reverence for the dead had given way to the corrupt and depressing effect of living in a place where hatred, dying, and fear had almost replaced the love of God and neighbor. Tears slipped down her face as she realized how fiercely she had come to love this valley before the war ravaged the foundations of its life.

Feeling that the sadness of Falling Water Valley was concentrated here, she walked through the overgrown cemetery. In her melancholy mood, the early morning dew wetting her long skirt symbolized the tears of the valley people for the life that had been torn from them.

She stood in front of a tiny rounded stone that bore the name of a woman who died in 1802. Viciously, she jerked out weeds surrounding the stone. How could the people of the valley let their anger with each other keep them from caring for the graves of their ancestors? What was this war doing to everyone?

Her quiet tears turned to open sobs as she tugged at the weeds. Maybe the fatigue that she felt spreading through her body, maybe the reaction to all that had happened in the past two days, were telling on her now, but the tears were healing. She found a spike of blue heal-all mint growing in the grasses and laid it on the stone. Somehow it made her feel better.

She stood before it for a moment, then turned and forced herself to stride off toward the road. That man inside was one of those who kept this valley a place of anger and violence instead of the peaceful and prosperous place it was when she and her father came here. He deserved only her care as a healer and no more. How could she feel such a desire to look in on him once more before she left?

Instead of going directly home, she stopped off at Bertie's small cabin. Bertie was up, standing beside the fireplace in her coarse shapeless gown, though the bedclothes hadn't been straightened. The emptiness in her face had been replaced with something else. Was it pain from her filling breasts or was it anger?

Tabitha was the only one with her. She stood close behind Bertie, hands on her shoulders, consoling or restraining her.

"I'm glad you've come, Bethany," Tabitha called, as Bethany stepped into the open doorway. "We need a reasonable voice here."

"What is it?" Bethany asked.

"What indeed?" Tabitha answered. "Just that some people in this valley have forgotten their Christianity and are listening to the evil mouthings of that old woman on the mountain."

"She knows." Bertie pulled herself from Tabitha's hands, her lips pulled back in a way that reminded Bethany of an angry dog. "She came down and told us that there's a man in the valley that shouldn't be here and he's taken Baby. . .Sally. She sees him with her second sight."

"But she doesn't see him quite good enough to tell us where he might be hiding," Tabitha said sarcastically. "Or where Baby is."

Bethany almost forgot to breathe. So Mattie was carrying

out her threats. But how could she be saying that the man in the church had Baby? He wasn't even capable of taking care of himself. But, of course, truth didn't mean anything to Mattie.

Truth? How much did truth mean to herself? Was she harming anyone by caring for the man in the church and keeping him a secret from the men of the valley? But if she told them now, what would they do to the man? *God, why is it sometimes so hard to know what to do?*

She almost saw the words on her father's letter. "I treat all who are brought to me for we are all God's children."

Bethany soothed Bertie as best she could and talked her into eating a little and drinking a cup of herbal tea. Then she left. She was too emotionally upset to feel she could help anyone else.

seven

"The only thing I can do is find Baby," she said to herself, hurrying up to her cabin. "But how am I going to do that? And why do I feel so reluctant to see that man in the church go away without knowing who he is?"

Bethany shook her head, admitting to herself that she had no plan for finding Baby Sally that the others weren't already using. The only possibility might come through her medicine. Mattie had to have attention to whatever injury she had to her leg. Maybe there was some bit of humanity hidden inside her that Bethany could touch by offering her medical help, that would cause her to tell if she had any real information about Baby Sally. Even if she didn't, she still needed treatment for that leg.

She decided that if Mattie hadn't come down to the cabin by the time she got home, she would take her saddlebags back up the mountain.

"God," she prayed, "help me to see her as just someone who needs help, not someone who is trying to hurt us."

Bethany sighed. She knew God heard but how could she ever stop feeling so frightened about what Mattie might do to that man in the church? Would she send the men looking for Baby Sally in there? So far, they'd never thought to look in there, or at least if they had, they had only opened the door and seen nothing. They were still searching over the valley and up in the mountain as well as they could with the few able-bodied men available.

She sighed. All she seemed to have were questions.

Another, more practical question came to her mind. Was Dave Bradley's leg well enough to be helping them search? She reminded herself to ask Nell if he had come in to have his dressings changed. Then she allowed her mind to return to her plans to talk to Mattie again.

There was no indication that Mattie had come to the cabin for treatment. Nell wasn't even there. Her medical saddlebags and Chief were gone and Bethany breathed a sigh of relief. She was sure that Nell would raise determined objections to her going back up the mountain.

Remembering that she had skipped breakfast, Bethany ate some cold bread spread with a spoonful of Nell's cottage cheese that she found on the table by the fireplace. Then she went out to the stable.

"Rainbow, do you mind one more climb?" she asked, rubbing the docile animal's nose, before she slipped on the bridle and saddle. Rainbow nibbled at her shoulder then stood quietly as she mounted and they set off up the mountain, through the blaze of sunlight on colorful autumn leaves.

Mattie was sitting at the same place she had been before in front of her hut with her left foot on the rock, and her right leg propped on a rotting log beside it. Bethany judged that whatever sore was on the leg must be getting worse.

"So you decided to listen to me," Mattie called as Bethany dismounted.

Bethany loosened Rainbow's reins and dropped them. She removed her saddlebags before replying.

"I've come to treat your leg, since you didn't come down to us," she said evenly.

Mattie looked away. "Told you I don't take charity," she said sullenly.

"All right. Pay me," Bethany answered practically.

"You know I ain't got no money."

"Well, what have you got?"

"Got nothing you can use if you won't let me deevine who that man is for you," Mattie said. "And after I deevined where he is now, too, but I haven't told the men down in the valley yet."

"Mattie, I know that you saw Willie and me carry that man into the church."

Mattie refused to meet her eyes. *Why, she acts like a spoiled child,* Bethany thought. Or maybe a hurt child. She let herself wonder what kind of a childhood Mattie had had. But she decided not to let her play any more games with her.

"Are you going to show me your leg?" she asked.

"It's just a little thing. I don't really need you," Mattie said. She stuck out her left leg and pulled up the skirt she wore to show a recent briar scratch. Bethany caught a glimpse of the calf of the right leg. She couldn't see anything there and considered that the wound must be on her thigh.

"Mattie, that scratch wouldn't make you limp like you do and you limp with that right leg. Let me see that one."

Mattie scowled. "Why do you care? I'm nothin' to you."

"You are something to me, Mattie. You're a child of God, though you may be acting like a child of Satan now. And you need help."

"Don't need help from no one. You ain't gonna let me deevine for you; you just go on down to that friend of yours."

"Nell?"

"No, don't mean Nell. Mean that man in the church."

"The bushwhacker?"

"He ain't no bushwhacker. I watched. I saw them come in. They had him tied on a horse and he'd already been beat up when they dumped him. The valley men didn't do it. They don't even know he's here. Not yet, anyway." Her eyes shot a threat to Bethany.

Bethany drew in a surprised breath and tried not to let her

relief show. So the man hadn't been a part of the raid on the valley. Then she shook her head at all the thoughts that rushed in. If the bushwhackers brought him in, he still must be connected with them in some way. Maybe he was one of them who had done something to make them angry. She turned back to Mattie.

"Will you let me see your leg?" she asked again.

"No." Mattie stood and walked away. Bethany could see that she was trying hard not to limp but not quite succeeding.

The leg concerned her but she accepted that, until Mattie agreed to let her treat it, there was nothing she could do.

"If you change your mind, come down to the cabin," she called after the other woman's broad back.

Mattie didn't respond but disappeared into the trees. Bethany watched her for awhile, then put her saddlebag on Rainbow and swung herself up. It was already after noon and she wanted to tell Nell about Mattie's latest threats as soon as possible.

Going back down the mountain, she let her mind rest on the man in the church. She forced herself to admit that Nell was right. No matter why he had been left in Falling Water Valley, they had to get him out for his own safety. With the uproar over the missing baby and the anger that grew with every bushwhacker raid, the valley men would take their passions out on this man. And Mattie knew where he was. She might tell them at any time.

Nell was at home when Bethany stabled Rainbow and went in. As expected, the older woman was upset that Bethany had gone back up the mountain. She wasn't at all sympathetic about Mattie's needs.

"She has to come down off her high horse and accept what we can give her if we're to help." Then she turned her attention to the man in the church.

"He's got to be taken out of the valley. It isn't just Mattie," she said. "Now that he's awake part of the time and eating he'll be going out to relieve himself. He could wander off or someone see him and who knows what they'd do with any stranger now, especially since Mattie is telling them that a stranger has the baby. We'll go down as soon as it starts to get dark," she added.

Bethany looked at the tall clock on the log mantle above the fireplace. "But that's at least four hours," she moaned. "What might happen to him before then?"

"Not as much as will happen to him if we try to take him out of the valley in daylight," Nell said practically.

Bethany had to agree. She busied herself building up the fire in the fireplace to heat up the rest of the dried bean soup Nell had made. Trying not to think of never getting to know the stranger in the church, she turned her mind to Mattie.

"Who is Mattie?" she asked Nell. "How did she end up living up on the top of the mountain trying to get people to come to her to find things for them? Do you think she's possessed by Satan?"

Nell snorted. "She's possessed by the need to be important," she said. "Not that Satan isn't glad to give someone like her a helping hand. She moved up on the mountain after her father died in a coma from the moonshine he made. Some say she may have helped him along. He was mean to her, beat her sometimes, especially after her mother died. But there wasn't enough evidence to make anyone take her to the law. It was just gossip. But the valley people didn't have much to do with her, though some of the women from the church tried to help. She just disappeared one day and, several months later, showed up on the mountain, pretending to be able to 'deevine' things. That was more than twenty years ago. People mostly just ignored her, but now that we've let this awful war turn us away from our Christian feelings for each other, it looks like some are listening to her."

Bethany felt tears in her eyes as she listened. "I have so

much to be thankful for," she whispered. "Daddy never took his hurt out on me. He always loved me."

"He's a loving man," Nell said, her voice soft, "though he found it hard sometimes to love God after his hurt."

Bethany held up the wooden spoon she was using to stir the soup. The thought burst full bloom into her mind, *Nell is in love with Daddy and he must have talked out his hurt and doubts to her.*

"You're dripping on the rug," Nell said shortly. Bethany understood that she was sorry she had let her feelings show.

Bethany turned back to the soup. She wasn't going to embarrass Nell by forcing her to admit anything, but how she wished that her father could return Nell's love.

She reached for the ladle hanging on a hook by the fireplace and filled two bowls. Bethany set them on the table and pulled out two corn cakes from the iron spider that had kept hot in the ashes, reached to a shelf above the table for two spoons, and settled herself across the table from Nell.

"Tomorrow you're going to have to cook something besides soup," Nell said, accepting the spoon and dipping it into the bowl. "I think a bit of that ham that Ruth Chisholm brought up after I spent the night with her croupy child might go very well."

Bethany nodded, knowing that she wasn't required to respond. If she could only wait until night to go back down to the church. Then it suddenly hit her. She hadn't even thought about plans or how they would spirit that man out of the valley.

She laid down her spoon. "Oh, I wish Willie hadn't run off to join the Union. Nell, how are we going to do this?"

"Do what?" Nell kept on placidly spooning soup into her mouth. "Wouldn't a cup of real coffee taste good now?" she asked.

Bethany stood up. "I'll heat up some of the ground acorn coffee. We can pretend it's real. But you haven't answered my question."

Nell let her spoon rest in the empty bowl. "Simple. He'll ride Rainbow. I'll ride Chief and I'll guide him over to Asheville. It'll be up to him to remember something or find a place to hide or whatever he can do there. He won't be our problem anymore."

Bethany felt a moment of remorse that the man would have to be dumped in Asheville, not knowing who he was or how to find help. She turned away from Nell, busying herself with the ersatz coffee to hide her feelings.

"I'll be gone about three days," Nell continued, not noticing Bethany's reaction. "You'll have to let people believe that I've gone over to Deer Ridge Valley to help out with a woman in hard labor."

"Why can't I. . .?"

"Because when your father comes back I don't plan to have to tell him that I let you leave here with someone who may be an outlaw and certainly is a stranger and has too much appeal to you, even if we knew anything about him."

"Nell!" Bethany jumped and some of the counterfeit coffee spilled out of the mug she was placing on the table.

Nell placidly wiped the spill with a bit of cloth. "Bethany, you need to get a good night's sleep tonight," she said gently. "You're so jumpy."

eight

"I'm going to get the horses ready now," Bethany said. She had been walking restlessly from window to door, watching for the daylight to fade.

Nell nodded. They had spent some of the time getting food and water ready for the trip to Asheville, and she was refilling their saddlebags.

The horses were both so gentle and cooperative that it never took long to get saddles and bridles on them, and Bethany and Nell were soon ready to start down to the church.

"We'll take the lantern for you to use walking back," Nell said. "Chief can guide the man and me out of the valley in the dark."

"Nell, I'm not sure my father would be any more pleased with you going off with a stranger than for me."

Nell shrugged. "There's no other way. This is a time when people have to do things they wouldn't ordinarily think of doing. If Willie were here we'd send him, but I wouldn't trust any other man in the valley right now. Or do you think we should depend on Dave Bradley?" Nell's voice told Bethany what her answer to that question would be.

"I don't know. I. . .guess I hadn't even thought of him," Bethany admitted.

"Shows what a sensible girl you are." Nell nodded emphatically. "If he was a real man, he'd be out of here in one army or another."

"Oh, Nell. . ." Bethany stopped. Though she had no reason

to suspect Dave of cowardice, she didn't want to waste their time talking about him.

She was more involved with her own guilt. If she hadn't insisted on Willie helping her get a strange man into the closed church, and keeping it a secret, he might have waited to join the Union army. Anyway, Nell wouldn't be on this dangerous mission tonight. Would she ever resolve her feelings about this man?

Her guilt turned to alarm as they guided the horses out onto the road. A lone man on a horse blocked their way. Her spirit sank as she recognized the bulk of Dave Bradley in the twilight.

"Well," he called, with a hint of seriousness under his cheery voice. "How am I ever going to court you properly, Bethany, if you keep going off on that horse of yours?"

Nell jerked Chief's reins to go around him and stop. A gentle tug on Rainbow's reins brought her to a stop in front of Dave as Bethany tried desperately to think of something to send him on his way without suspicion.

Gratefully, she heard Nell's sharp voice. "And do you have permission from Bethany's father to court her?"

"That's a little hard to do since he's gone to keep the Yanks alive after we try to pepper their backs and chase them out of our land." Dave's voice had lost its cheerfulness.

Neither woman bothered to correct him as to where Dr. Andrews was serving. Like many in the valley, Dave often let his prejudices shape what he chose to believe.

"Aren't you a little quick to say 'we,' Dave Bradley?" Nell called back. "I don't see a uniform on you, blue or gray."

"You know that some of us have to stay and protect the valley," he said. Bethany recognized an unusual seriousness in his voice and remembered that he was considered to be the quickest one out to try to chase off the bushwhackers when they raided.

"Men with families. Older men." Nell seemed determined to anger Dave. Bethany remained silent, wondering if Nell was only maneuvering for time or perhaps trying to make him shamed or angry enough to leave them.

"Part of the need is to protect young. . ." he cast an infuriated look at Nell, ". . .girls who are taken out into dangerous roads by a crazy old woman. Especially now when Mountaintop Mattie is seeing a stranger in the valley somewhere. So, wherever you're going, Bethany, I'm going with you."

"Well, someone who listens to old Mountaintop Mattie isn't much of a protector," Nell called.

"You know Mattie sees a lot," Dave answered, without saying whether he meant with her physical eyes, but Bethany thought he probably did. She knew him well enough to know that he wouldn't really believe Mattie's nonsense about second sight.

"I'm going with you, Bethany," he insisted.

Desperately, Bethany searched her mind for somewhere to take him. Maybe if she led him off, Nell could continue down to the church and get the stranger out.

"We're going to stop in on Bertie to see how she's doing. You're welcome to come with us."

She thought she heard an impatient sigh from Nell, but Dave turned his horse aside to let her pass. As she caught up with Nell, she heard him pulling his horse in behind her.

"Dave. Dave. Is that you?" The hail came from someone riding around from in back of the cabin. As he pulled his horse up, Bethany recognized Willie's Uncle Dannel Bowers.

"Dave," he called excitedly, "we're going up to get Mattie to tell us where the MacMillan baby is. Rance Miller says she's had a 'seeing' and will take us directly to that stranger who has her. Come with us."

Nell and Bethany watched as Dave lost his desire to protect them in the possibility of getting involved with a rescue of the baby, as well as finding out what some strange man might be doing in the valley. Bethany shuddered, thinking of what they would do to that man if they found him. The beating he had already taken would be as nothing to what their fear would force them to do. This time he would be killed.

"We think the man may have holed up in that cave where we found the bear. If he was watching us, he'd figure we wouldn't search it again any time soon. Mattie may have seen him," they heard Dannel say as they drove their horses toward the base of the mountain. "Did you bring your gun?"

"Well," Nell said in a low tone, "maybe even Mattie is good for something since she made Dave leave."

"Nell, I can't believe that Dave and Dannel believe Mattie's nonsense. They're Christians."

"They seemed to be," Nell acknowledged. "So many people are changing. We can see now how much we need our church. It's a sad, sad time. But Dave was never the man for you, Bethany. Some things just weren't meant to be. Anyway, we need to think about our own plans now."

"Oh, Nell, what have I done? Now we have to stop at Bertie's house to keep me from lying."

"Don't worry, Bethany. Maybe it's just as well. My bones tell me that Dave's concern about protecting you wasn't as real as a yen to see where we're going. They may have someone watching us now. We'll just stop at Bertie's and throw them off if they do."

"Why should they suspect us of anything? Do you think that Mattie's really been telling them anything true about this man? Surely she couldn't after I tried to help her."

"Mattie could. Or she may be hinting just enough to keep them coming up to her. But, whatever game she's playing, she's giving us some help, though I'm sure it's not out of any friendly feelings. She's leading them away from the church to go hear whatever she wants to tell them now."

"But we can't count on her not telling them tonight. Let's not stay long at Bertie's."

They found Virgie Smith taking her turn to stay with Bertie. She greeted them warmly. "I was just making Bertie and me a cup of dandelion tea. Sit down and take these. I'll pour two more cups."

Instinctively, Bethany put out a hand to take the cup Virgie pressed on her and sank into a chair by the fireside where Bertie sat huddled in a blanket. Nell sat on Bertie's other side, giving Bethany a slight frown and shake of her head that told her she was letting her uneasiness show. She took in several deep breaths and tried to concentrate on drinking the slightly bitter tea, while Nell talked comfortingly with Bertie.

It seemed hours before they could put down their cups and say good night, admonishing Bertie to try to get some sleep.

"Nell, I've made us waste so much time," Bethany whispered, as they closed the door behind them and stepped out into the darkness.

"Don't fret, Bethany. We're doing the best we can," Nell replied, leading the way to the horses. "We'll get him up and on Rainbow as quick as we can. I just hope he's awake and strong enough to ride."

As before, they went off the road before they reached the lane to the church, and left Rainbow and Chief tied to bushes behind it.

"Let me hang this over the window before you light the lantern," Nell said, as they slipped around the side of the church to the front door. She indicated a fox skin she carried. "We'd best not let any light show to anyone tonight."

After Nell had tucked the skin closely about the nails that used to hold a beautifully embroidered curtain on the window of the church, Bethany lit the lantern. Automatically, she first shone the dim light on the spot before the benches where the man had been lying.

"Oh, no," she whispered, "we're too late. He's gone. They've found him."

"I don't think so," Nell answered in a normal voice. "Look up there."

It took a minute for Bethany to realize that the man stood behind the pulpit, silently watching them, but looking almost as if he were quietly waiting for an audience to settle down so he could deliver a sermon.

Nell took the lantern and strode to stand before the pulpit, holding the light high. "Well, I see you're standing, though I have strong doubts about you standing in the place where our preacher used to."

He stared at the light for awhile. Then he looked at Nell. "I'm not aware of your minister, but I feel very much at home standing here. I can almost remember. . .parts of names run through my mind."

Bethany gasped and felt a shiver of delight run through her. If he felt at home in the pulpit. . .if he was a minister. . .he couldn't be one of the bushwhackers. She didn't take the time to question the rush of joy. Maybe it was just the joy of thinking he was a Christian. She left it at that.

Nell didn't seem to be impressed. "Whatever you do or don't remember, I'm taking you out to Asheville tonight. What you do after that is up to you."

Something in the man seemed to stir. Something that told Bethany he was used to planning his own paths. For a minute, she had the impression of the fire of an evangelist as he looked down on them.

"No." The one word was firm.

Nell's almost angry look echoed Bethany's surprise. They were keyed up from all the trouble they had gone through to get to the church. The last thing they had expected was for him not to follow their decisions without questioning them. After all, if he really didn't know who he was or how he got into the valley, he surely would be glad for them to get him out.

He stood silently, wandering through the haze of his mind to find his reason for refusing their offer. Was it just the wish to get to know the woman named Bethany better or was it something else. . .something deeper. . .something he'd been struggling with for a long time. . .trying to accomplish? And why could he remember Bethany's name, a name he had only overheard the other woman use, when he couldn't remember his own?

"Don't you understand anything?" Nell argued. "Don't you know that you could be killed if the men of the valley knew you were here? And they may be coming close to learning about you. Don't you even remember that there's a war going on? It's killing the decency in people just as sure as it's killing men on the battlefield. Neighbors fighting against neighbors, people that used to be friends, willing to help each other out, hating and doing downright dirty work against each other, sneaking around. . ."

"You people need to remember love. You need to remember love of country, love of each other, love of God, who looks down on us while we fight across His beautiful land. . ."

His hands gripped the edges of the rough podium and his long upper body leaned across it as though his body remembered a position his mind had forgotten.

Bethany reacted to his words and the fire in his dark eyes with emotion of her own. Love, country, God. Words she hadn't heard from a pulpit since the furies of the war had entered the pleasant valley, like an evil spirit, to close their church.

"You're talking mighty like a preacher, friend," Nell's voice deepened as she flung the words at him. Silently, Bethany watched the confrontation in the amber light, somehow thinking of an Old Testament prophet challenging a king.

"Now dig down into that mind of yours," Nell continued.

"Show me proof or get away from that pulpit. I demand to know your name and what you did that got you in here."

"We can settle this without killing each other. This country belongs to all of us. We can rid ourselves of the onus of that ugly institution of slavery without tearing our country's heart out."

He stopped talking and looked down at Nell, so close to the podium that she was directly below him. Bethany realized that she was involuntarily holding her breath.

This was between the stranger and Nell. She seemed to be physically drawing the truth out of him, as their intent gazes locked across the short space between them.

"Joshua. . .June. . ." The words fell like strewn marbles into the silence.

Bethany sat down, her mind numbed with disappointment. He had only remembered two names, one of them a woman's. What had she hoped for? That she would be rewarded for her Good Samaritan performance by finding the man she had sometimes dreamed of? A man that, up until now, looked a lot like this man?

He did look at home up there behind that pulpit, and he didn't look like a bushwhacker. She had to admit that, standing up, he looked to be in his early thirties, plenty old enough to have a wife. . .maybe several children.

Never mind. He still needed her help. Hers and Nell's.

But he was talking again.

"Asheville. I preached there. I know I did." He hesitated and a frown appeared between his brown eyes. "I. . .don't know if I live there. . .I don't know. . .perhaps I have no home."

"Was it in Asheville that you got that knot on your head? And those bruises?"

He stood before Nell, but he looked at Bethany. "I. . .don't know. I rode, holding church wherever I could get people together to hear the Word of God and of peace. . .everyone is so angry. . . Sometimes I've been run out of places where I've tried to preach. I. . .think I was pulled off my horse. . .I don't know what happened."

Bethany stood up in her excitement. "They must have beat you up and left you here, thinking that if you didn't die, the men of the valley would kill you for a bushwhacker."

Nell suddenly whirled around and stood listening for a minute. "There's someone coming," she said briefly. "We'd better hide you."

nine

"Come over here. Just lie down here in front of the benches, where you were." Frantically, Nell stepped behind the pulpit and pushed against him.

Surprised and confused, Joshua allowed her to force his tall body to the floor.

The church door opened slowly, as though whoever was there was unsure about coming in, or hoped to take them by surprise. Bethany and Nell stood motionless, barely breathing. The door stopped briefly, moved again, then opened.

Bethany was the first to react as the thin, white-haired man stepped falteringly into the dim light.

"Daddy," she whispered. Then louder, all the love and happiness of seeing him sounding in her voice. "Daddy."

Her mind suddenly crowded with memories of all the times she had felt the happy comfort of waking in the night and hearing him come in from a late-night call to a sick neighbor. For a minute, as she ran to him, she was a tiny child again, left with a housekeeper in one of the many houses where they had lived, but not able to sleep until he came home.

In spite of the affection that filled his eyes at the sight of her, he put out a hand to hold her off. Her breath caught as she realized that his shockingly thin body was near collapse. She stopped the exuberant hug she wanted to give him and, instead, returning to being a young woman, slipped a supportive arm gently around him.

"Daddy, come sit down," she said, almost holding him

upright as she guided him to the closest bench.

Nell hurried down the aisle toward them. Her face showed that she had forgotten all about the stranger and her only concern was for Ben Andrews.

"Whatever is it, Ben?" she asked, sitting down on the other side of him, and taking his weight off Bethany. "You're nothing but a bag of bones, collapsing into yourself."

In spite of his pain and fatigue, Ben Andrews managed an affectionate smile. "You haven't lost any of your bent for excessive flattery, Nell," he said, in a hoarse and strangely tight voice, as though he was pushing it from some water-filled cave inside him. He made an attempt to sit up straight, then let his body slump against her. "I can't tell you how glad I was to see Chief and Rainbow. I'm not sure I could have made it home."

Bethany suddenly remembered the man lying at the front of the church. "You saw our horses? We thought we had put them out of sight of the road."

Ben looked at her in surprise. ". . .Probably are out of sight of the road. . .dark as it is. I came in through the trees. It was shorter."

"Ben Andrews, are you walking?"

Ben nodded. "I started riding. . .someone with a gun took my horse. Don't know if he was Reb or Union."

"Probably bushwhacker," Nell said. Then she called without looking, "Joshua, you can come out now. This is a friend."

"Of course." Joshua spoke from just beside them.

He probably didn't wait much for permission to do anything, Bethany thought. At least not permission from anyone but God. Then she introduced her father, stumbling over using just the name Joshua. Her father looked intently at the man.

"Brother Holt. Heard you preach once. . .before the army. What you said made. . .good sense. People should. . .have listened. Heard. . .a lot of people didn't like what you were saying." His voice was becoming fainter, hoarser each time he spoke.

Bethany leaned away from her father for a moment, not wanting him to feel her body suddenly shaking with intense relief. Now they knew for sure that the man called Joshua wasn't a bushwhacker. He was a man of God.

In spite of her concern for her father, Bethany felt a smile tugging at her mouth. She had heard Joshua Holt talked about. The minister who spoke God's truth in spite of threats from angry men. Men who were taking their anger at the tragic war out on anyone who told them they shouldn't let it make them lose their neighborly love for each other. It was a forlorn circle of emotion.

If hearing his last name gave Joshua a desire to ask for more information he fought it back, in concern for the sick man. He bent his tall body toward Ben.

"I hope to talk with you about this later. But, even I can see that you need to have these two healers do for you what they did for me."

Ben looked a question at them.

"Never mind," Nell said briskly. "Ben, before we even try to tell you how glad we are to see you, we'll get you up to the cabin to bed. Bethany, get on that side of him. We'll get him on Rainbow and I'll walk beside him. The way he looks now, he might fall off." She touched her palm to his forehead. "Running a mighty high fever, too. What is it, Ben?"

Almost as if in answer, Ben suddenly curled up with a fit of coughing, holding his chest as though each cough brought agony. Bethany caught him to herself as tightly as she dared, longing to be able to send strength from her own healthy body into his.

"Never mind. I can see you've got pneumonia, no matter what else happened. We'll get you warmed and some beef tea in you and a turpentine poultice on that chest."

Ben nodded. "It's been a long way home," he said in a near whisper.

Bethany wondered if his last words meant more than just his physical journey. But, like Nell, she wanted to get him up to the cabin, warmed, fed, cared for. It was obvious that now he'd found them he was letting himself slip rapidly into a semiconscious state.

Nell, ignoring the fact that their light might be seen, jerked the fox skin from the window and placed it around Ben's trembling shoulders.

"Bethany," she said, briskly, "we'll have to lift him onto Chief and one of us ride behind him. He's too far gone to help us any."

Joshua quickly stepped forward. "I'll do it."

Before either of them could stop him, he had picked the frail body up in his arms and strode toward the door. He staggered once but he didn't stop.

"Joshua, no. You mustn't be seen," Bethany called. She picked up the lantern and followed them.

He paid no attention, only stopping long enough at the door for Nell to guide him toward the horses. Nell seemed to be too intent on Ben's needs to consider that Joshua might be in danger or in pain. She held Ben against her own body while Joshua struggled into Chief's saddle.

Then, all working together, they managed to get Ben up in front of him, his legs swinging off to the side while Joshua held him with both arms under his and the slumping body nestled against his own.

Not knowing where to guide the horse, he let the reins lie loosely on Chief's neck. Chief followed Nell, who strode off ahead of them, carrying the lantern.

Bethany picked up Rainbow's reins and swung herself astride, her wide skirts settling as usual about her legs. Her mind was a battlefield of emotions. She whispered her gratitude to God that her father had come home and a fervent prayer for his recovery.

But mixed in was a confusion of fear for Joshua's safety and thankfulness that he wasn't a bushwhacker, but someone she could respect. Layered over all was a question of why she should be so happy about that.

Of course she was glad that he was a minister but he probably had a wife and family somewhere, even if he didn't remember anything but the name, June. The way his memories were returning, he surely would remember them soon and want to go home to them. And she would need to be glad for him. Of course she would be glad for them. All of them.

And, anyway, he was someone she had only known for such a little while. *Not nearly long enough to have any feelings about,* she said firmly to herself. But the half-joking courting of Dave Bradley had never brought out any of the emotions she was having to fight against now.

Watching the tall figure in the saddle going slowly in front of her in the flickering pale blur of the lantern Nell carried, she felt a rush of blood to her face.

Bethany Andrews, you're going strange on us, she scolded herself.

They met no one on the road and saw no lights in the cabins strewn about the valley. Bethany wondered if the men who had ridden up the mountain were still there or if they were disappointed in what Mattie had to say and had gone back to their homes. She prayed that they wouldn't suddenly come thundering down out of the trees onto their little cavalcade.

She judged that it must be about ten o'clock and that most of the families were in bed. Even Bertie must have given up and gone to sleep for there was not even the glow of a fireplace in her cabin beside the road.

Nell led them up to the front door of their cabin and helped get Ben down. They let the horses find their own way to the barn while they concentrated on getting Ben across the porch and into the cabin.

Again Joshua insisted on carrying him, though Bethany was uneasily aware that he struggled under the slight weight. Nell directed him to lay Ben down on Bethany's own bed. While he removed Ben's dirty clothes, Nell bustled about building up the fire and warming flannel for a poultice to his chest.

The three of them cooperated on taking care of him as though they had worked together before. Bethany rummaged for extra covers and soft flannel underwear in the chest that she and her father had carried from place to place. Joshua dressed him in the comfortingly fresh clothes and spread the extra blankets on him.

Bethany took the piece of dried beef that Nell brought out from somewhere, put it into their iron pot, and hung it over the fire. Strengthening beef broth would be ready when her father became awake enough to drink it. As she turned from the fireplace, she felt the length of Joshua's body close beside her.

She stepped backward quickly and stumbled. Immediately, she felt the steady comfort of his hand against her back, keeping her from falling. He held it there only long enough to steady her, but she seemed to feel the warmth even after he moved it.

"Are you all right?" he asked.

Such ordinary words. And words she should be saying to him. Why did she find them so comforting? She looked up at him and found his gaze meeting hers with compassion and something she couldn't quite name, which left her feeling a shivering warmth clear down to her toes.

"Well, now we don't have to worry about getting you out of the valley anymore." Nell's words brought them abruptly back to the problems of Joshua's situation. They both turned questioning eyes toward her.

"Don't you see?" she continued, hardly looking up from rubbing warm turpentine well diluted with fat on Ben's chest, "you are a Good Samaritan who helped Ben get home. That's no lie, you know. No matter who you are, you have a reason to be here. And," she added, "now that Ben's recognized you, we do know who you are."

Bethany's own thoughts about playing the Good Samaritan raced through her mind. She dared a sideways look at Joshua, who was only looking in amused distraction at Nell.

Nell came to the fireplace and picked up a large piece of heated flannel, which she folded and tucked loosely about Ben's chest.

"Joshua, you can sleep in my bed," she added in a no-nonsense tone, seating herself beside Ben. "I'll stay in here with Bethany and Ben. You'll be a great help to us after you rest. You're still a patient, you know. But I reckon helping us with Ben won't be any harder on you than riding to Asheville."

Bethany didn't question her plans. Joshua didn't have to leave. She reminded herself again that she mustn't allow herself to feel anything other than a Christian response to his need.

Though she felt sure that he wouldn't intentionally hide it from them if he knew who June was, eventually he would remember. And a name that stayed with him when even his own last name didn't had to be the name of someone very important to him.

Still, growing up close to her father and with the simple people of the mountains, she had learned to disregard the pretenses of city women and to be honest with herself. She was glad to be able to get to know Joshua Holt better, even though there could be nothing between them. The name June prohibited it.

ten

Joshua didn't object to Nell's direction that he go to bed in Ben's old room, where she now slept and saw patients. Bethany could see that lifting Ben and riding behind him up to their cabin had taken its toll on his recovering body. He moved laboriously as he went through the door to the adjoining room, and several times she had seen an expression of pain on his bruised face.

Once he was gone, Nell proceeded to make up a pallet on the floor in front of the fireplace for Bethany. She refused to listen to Bethany's reluctance to sleep.

"There's no need for both of us to stay up all night, and I'm not leaving Ben's bedside." This time she made no effort to hide her feelings for him, and Bethany gave in to her and her own exhausted body. She was barely aware of Nell moving about the room, though she heard her father coughing as if in a dream.

A pale light had filled the cabin when she woke and tiptoed over to Ben's bed. Nell was nodding, but she came abruptly awake when she felt Bethany beside her.

"How is he?" Bethany whispered.

Nell shook her head. "I've been sponging him but I can't get that fever down. I've got a little boneset tea into him, though, to make him sweat."

Ben opened his eyes and reached a thin hand toward Bethany. Bethany took it in both her own and brought it to her face, covering it equally with kisses and tears.

"Daddy, I've missed you so. You have to get well now."

He managed a small smile, started to say something, but was stopped by a spell of coughing. The pain of it wrenched his face as he pulled his hand from Bethany's and pressed it against his chest.

"Here, hold this pillow against it," Nell said. Ben took the pillow from her with a grateful look. After the cough quieted down, he slumped against the bed. It seemed to Bethany that his body collapsed into the feather mattress, barely making a mound under the blankets.

"I'll stay with him now," she whispered to Nell. "You have to rest."

Ben opened his eyes. "Don't whisper around the patient," he whispered himself, ". . .taught you. . ."

"Oh, Daddy, I forgot. I just didn't want to wake you."

". . .Not awake. . .not since you and Nell. . .helped me."

He drifted off again and Bethany sat down beside him without trying to remind him of the help that Joshua Holt had given them. She reflected for a moment on placing the name with the man who had been so much a part of the last hours.

Nell went to the fireplace. "This beef broth is ready now. It's been cooking all night. I'm going to put some out to cool, and you've got to get him to take some even if you have to wake him up. What about our kindly stranger who brought him home? Have you heard anything from the other room?"

Bethany shook her head.

"I'll go see if he's still with us," Nell said.

"Of course I'm still with you." The door opened and Joshua stood there. "You're my rescuers. I intend to stay around and make myself as helpful as possible."

"Fine. The first thing you can do is get us some more wood. We'll have to keep this fire going all day, even if it warms up outside. We've got to keep the beef broth hot and steep some sweet everlasting and more boneset for Ben. No, the first thing you do is eat some breakfast. We've got oatmeal. I cooked it a couple of days ago and it's warming near the fire."

"Good," Joshua said. "It gets better every time it's heated."

He took a bowl to the fireplace and served himself from the pot. He sat down at the table and ate it with obvious relish. Then after inquiring after Ben, he picked up the axe from its place beside the fireplace and went outside.

"Should we let him be seen, Nell?" Bethany asked. "And I worry about that rib." Nell wouldn't have let him go out with that axe if she wasn't so intent on Ben's needs.

"He should be able to judge how much he can do. He strikes me as someone who makes his own judgments. And remember, he's not a mystery man anymore. He's a kindly stranger. We can't act like he has to be hidden. And the people of the valley should be so happy to get their doctor back that they'll accept him."

"Unless Mattie decides to carry out her threat and tell everyone he's the one who took Baby Sally."

"We'll just have to take that chance. Even if she does, maybe people will have got back enough gumption not to believe her."

"Nell, after you've slept awhile, I need to go up and see if Mattie will let me treat that leg. I think she must have a bad injury to it."

Nell snorted. "I won't try to keep you from going. Maybe this time you'll find out where she's hiding Baby."

"You still think she took her, don't you?"

"Who else was out roaming around that night?"

"Just about everybody in the valley, if you remember."

Nell shrugged. "You're right. Now, don't forget to get that broth down Ben as soon as it cools down enough. And give him some of that sweet everlasting in about an hour. I'm going in to bed while it's still warm from the kindly stranger." Without looking back, Nell shut the door behind her.

Joshua brought in a small armful of wood, his unhappy expression telling Bethany that his bruises still hurt. He pulled a chair from the table to sit beside her.

All through the morning, Bethany stayed beside her father's bed while he drifted between sleep and fits of coughing. She only disturbed him to change the poultices on his chest, or slip spoonfuls of beef broth or herb teas into his limp mouth.

When Ben woke, Joshua helped her with him, otherwise he sat silently beside her. Much as Bethany longed to find out more about him, she appreciated his understanding of her father's need for quiet. And, she reflected, he probably needed quiet himself to ease his aching body and search inside his mind for returning memories. How would it feel not to know simple little everyday facts about yourself? Memories are so much of who a person is.

About noon, Nell woke and took her place beside Ben's bed. Speaking in a low tone, Bethany announced her intention to go up the mountain to try to convince Mattie to accept treatment for her leg. Nell nodded with approval when Joshua said he would go with her.

With Joshua mounted on Chief and Bethany on Rainbow, her medical saddlebags behind her, they started up the mountain, Rainbow leading.

It was a bright late October afternoon. The brilliant blue sky seemed sharp with color as though intensified by the reds and yellows of the trees.

About halfway up the mountain, the trail widened enough for Joshua to pull Chief up beside Rainbow.

"Bethany, I know who I am now, at least I know my name and that I'm a circuit rider, but I still don't know where I am. This is a beautiful place, but not familiar to me. Can you tell me about it?"

"It's called Falling Water Valley," Bethany explained. "There's a waterfall back on this mountain on the stream that runs through the valley. It's just a little one, but the story is that the first settler here, in the late 1700s, saved his life hiding from angry Indians in a cave near the waterfall, so he named the valley after it. No one knows where the cave is now. I don't think anyone has even tried to find it recently."

"That's not unusual," Joshua commented. "These mountains are full of hidden caves."

"A lot of them around here have been checked out the past few days. A bear was pulled out of one and killed."

Bethany told him about the missing Baby Sally and explained that she suspected that the woman they were going to see might have the baby.

"I have to almost hope she has her. It's better than thinking some wild animal or the bushwhackers took her. Mattie comes down and slips around the valley without being seen, big as she is. She just knows the mountain and the valley so well that she can hide. Then she pretends to have visions about what is happening down there. . .where lost property is. . .that kind of thing. Most of the people in the valley ignore her, but there's always been a few who go up to her when something is lost. And now," Bethany added ruefully, "with the war and the anger all around us, more are beginning to listen to her."

She told him briefly about the men who halted Nell and her as they set out for the church the night before. Without conscious thought, she neglected to mention Dave Bradley's name.

"I wonder if Mattie's was the face that I dimly remember seeing above me in the church," Joshua mused. "Somewhere in my mind, I knew that there were more than just you kneeling above me."

"It probably was," Bethany agreed. "She knew you were there and made threats about you."

By the time she had explained, they came out into Mattie's clearing.

Mattie was sitting before her cabin, her right leg propped straight out in front of her on a short log as before. She was obviously in pain, but she greeted them with her usual show of confidence and independence.

"So. You've decided to show yourself now that Dr. Ben is back. Think he can protect you, sick as he is? I didn't tell anyone where you were last night but I still can." She peered intently at Joshua with her brilliant eyes. "That face don't look too good yet."

Bethany ignored her greeting and her own surprise that, painful as Mattie's leg was, she was still getting down the mountain to spy on the valley activities. She dismounted and took her supplies from her saddlebag.

"I came with Bethany, who only desires to treat your leg," Joshua answered quietly.

Mattie looked at Bethany, in a pathetic attempt to maintain control. "I don't take charity," she said.

Joshua stepped forward and moved her leg slightly and Mattie let out an involuntary moan.

"You can pay for the treatment by telling Bethany where you are keeping the baby," he said, with the authority of a minister in his voice.

Mattie gazed at him for a moment with resentment, then she shrugged. "Do what you can," she said, in a quiet voice Bethany had never heard from her before. "But you," her belligerence returned as she pointed to Joshua, "you leave. No man sees my legs."

Joshua answered her seriously and with respect for her surprising modesty. "I'll walk over and watch the light change on the oaks below. But I'll be easily in hearing if you should need me."

Mattie's look was almost one of gratitude. Bethany guessed that she had seldom received respect of any kind in her life. But she waited until Joshua had turned his back and moved away before she stood and pulled her tattered skirt almost to the top of her thigh.

Before she could change her mind, Bethany knelt beside her. The back of her thigh was hot and swollen. Bethany washed it carefully in a yarrow solution to numb the pain as much as possible, noting at the time that the leg was clean. *Mattie must wash in the creek,* she thought.

A quick examination showed that the problem was from a piece of dirty rock that had been imbedded in the leg for some time. Ordinarily, she was sure, Mattie would have taken care of such a thing herself, but this was in such a place on her large body that she couldn't see it well.

"I'm going to have to open it and get that out," she said, taking Ben's lancet out of the saddlebag. "It's going to hurt. It would be best if you lie down. May I get Joshua to hold the leg still for me?"

"I don't need no one to hold me down for anything," Mattie growled. "Don't you bring him over here. And I don't need to lie down. I don't want anyone standing over me."

True to her word, Mattie didn't move or drop her skirt while Bethany made a quick stab into the festering flesh. The rock came out with a putrid drainage of pus and blood. In spite of herself, Mattie's sighs showed momentary pain, then relief as the agonizing pressure of corruption eased.

Bethany laid the lancet inside a small linsey square, to be washed when she got back down the mountainside. She washed the leg several times again, removing the discharge. Then she made a compress of lint soaked in a gentian solution and wrapped it firmly, the size of the leg causing her to use more of her spare store of cloth than she wanted to.

Then she rose. "I'll come back tomorrow to change the dressing," she said. "Then it should be healed enough for you to come down the mountain to our cabin."

Mattie didn't respond and Bethany moved off to replace

her saddlebags on Rainbow.

Mattie sat down on her stoop, her movements showing that she was still in pain. But she carefully replaced her tattered clothing.

"You can come back now," she called to Joshua.

At her summons, he walked back and stood beside her.

"Now you will pay Bethany," he said firmly. "Where do you have the baby?"

eleven

Mattie's expression changed to some emotion that Bethany couldn't quite interpret. "Bethany acted like a real Christian," she said, "coming up here and making my leg better. And you went away when I asked you to. I can't tell you exactly where the baby is right now but I make you a promise. If you'll go to the church this evening, just after dark, I promise you the baby'll be there and you can take her back to that bad mother of hers. But she don't deserve her back. She was mean to her, leaving her on the ground. Somebody had to save the baby from wild animals or bad men."

She looked Joshua directly in the eye, as though daring him to ask the obvious question of her, though they all knew that she had the baby hidden somewhere. Looking at her now, Bethany felt sure that the baby was receiving good care. Maybe better care than Mattie herself had received as a child.

Mattie refused to listen to their arguments that she take them to the baby. Instead, she insisted that her promise was the best she could do, and finally, afraid that they might cause her to go back on that promise, they gave up and mounted their horses. Bethany noticed that Joshua, instead of offering her unneeded help to mount, carefully looked away until she had settled her wide skirt modestly about Rainbow's saddle.

"Joshua, thank you for getting Mattie to promise us we can get the baby. How can I tell you how much it means?"

"I know how much a child means to her mother. As much as a childless man can understand. But it was your Christian giving of care even when she didn't seem to deserve it that made her give us that promise."

Bethany was riding in front of Joshua on a narrow part of the trail. She held the reins loosely and let Rainbow find her own way for a short while. Joshua had called himself a childless man without seeming to be aware of it. Was he remembering something else?

If he was, he didn't choose to talk about it. She pushed thoughts about his marital status out of her mind and returned to the emotions she had seen on Mattie's face.

Then Bethany turned in the saddle and looked back at Joshua. "It's hard to put into words, but Mattie responded to your kindness and respect for her privacy and again to your firmness. I have a strong sense that you have become important in her eyes."

"I hope I can help her. But she's been alone against the world for so long that she may fight my help, as well as God's."

Bethany maneuvered Rainbow back beside Chief, as the trail widened. "I understand that. My father spent my childhood trying to run away from the pain of losing my mother. He only recently seems to be learning that he can't get away from it that way." She briefly explained the way they moved from one place to another throughout her childhood.

"And did he cause you pain by carrying you from place to place?" he asked seriously, as though the answer was important to him.

. "I don't remember any other kind of life," Bethany answered thoughtfully, "so I suppose I don't know if I missed anything important. I knew he loved me and we were welcome wherever we went, so I never had a feeling of rejection. Sometimes I liked a place so much that I didn't want to leave," she added honestly. "Maybe I resented moving sometimes. I learned not to make any close friends."

Joshua didn't respond with any information he may have remembered about his own life and Bethany couldn't read his expression. He was looking straight ahead and she could only admire the straight-nosed profile that he showed to her. A stray thought that she was glad he had used her father's razor instead of letting his beard grow drifted through her mind.

He seemed to be concentrating on listening to the drum of a woodpecker back in the trees, but she had a strong feeling that he wasn't.

"That's a big one," he remarked, as though it were important. "Listen to him hammer."

She nodded, then realized that he still hadn't looked at her. Suddenly his hands jerked so strongly that Chief stopped.

"June."

Bethany pulled Rainbow to a standstill beside him, her chest hurting at the name.

"Your wife?" She had to know.

He shook his head. "I know who June is." He pointed to a little tree beside the trail.

Bethany looked at the tiny apple-shaped purplish fruit hanging on the tree. "Serviceberry," she murmured in confusion. She knew the uses of its bark, but they were too personal to mention and she had no idea why he was interested.

"We called it Shadbush and Juneberry, June and I. June's my sister, Bethany. My older sister. When we were children and I thought she was too bossy, I used to tell her she wasn't anything but a bug and a bush. And she'd yell that, no, she was June, June, June, and if she was anything besides a girl, she was something important—a month. Then she married a man named John and I used to call them the two Js."

He laughed in delight at the memory. "June's home is my base. She and John supported me and welcomed me when I could get there as long as John was home." He became serious again. "Now it's just her and her son since John has joined the

Confederate Army. But she still welcomes me, even though I can't pretend to support John's convictions, and he thinks I'm wrong to preach against the war. June doesn't tell me what she thinks of it. She just loves us both."

"Tell me about her," Bethany said, aware that she was only trying to cover the wild burst of relief to know who this June was. She insisted that Rainbow, who had realized she was getting closer to the stable and food, stay beside him.

At the request, he turned his face toward her and smiled. "She's like a mother, even though she's only five years older. Our parents both died a few years ago, and June has very seriously taken over Mother's job of worrying about whether I eat three times a day when I'm riding about the country."

"Do you?"

He grinned. "Actually, I think I do. Sometimes, I only eat once on each day between meetings, but when I go into a community, I'm fed at every house in one day, so it all averages out."

Bethany laughed with him, as much at sharing his gratification at his returning memories as at his comment.

He pulled Chief's head around and started him on down the mountainside. Bethany let Rainbow follow.

"While I was looking at the view from Mattie's place, I remembered my horse. Old Solomon. I just hope that Old Solomon found his way back somewhere where he'll be cared for after I was pulled off him."

They were in the valley now and Bethany let Rainbow have her head as she raced past Chief on her way to her stable.

"If he's as wise as his name, he must have," she called back to Joshua on the more dignified Chief. "Solomon knows where his oats are."

She loved the sound of Joshua's laughter behind her.

৯

"I wouldn't trust Mattie as far as I could throw a cow," Nell said practically, when they told her of their afternoon's work. "She's just lived in her hatred and pretense too long. Why didn't she give you Baby while you were up there?"

"Nell, people can change and they do," Bethany reminded her. "I'm not sure that she has the baby up there. Just that she knows where she is and she took her because she thought Bertie wasn't taking care of her. Remember, I've looked in her cabin and Baby Sally wasn't there."

They were standing in Nell's room where she had come in to talk to them without disturbing Ben.

"But why is she making you wait 'til dark to get the baby?" she asked.

"Maybe she thought it might not be safe for Joshua to go down there before dark. I know we're taking a chance, Nell, but we have to do it."

"Yes, we have a possibility of getting the baby back with her mother where she belongs," Joshua added.

Then, changing the subject, he asked about Ben. Nell shook her head. "There's no way to tell how long he's had the pneumonia, but he's getting to the point where the fever has to break if he's going to make it," she said. "I can't possibly leave him to go with you to the church."

"Oh, Nell, you know I don't want you to leave him," Bethany said, throwing her arms about her. "I just love you for taking such good care of him. You know I wouldn't leave him either, if it wasn't so important to get Baby Sally back." She didn't talk about her understanding of Nell's commitment to Ben.

Joshua looked thoughtful. "Perhaps you shouldn't leave him, either, Bethany. I can go to the church alone."

Bethany felt torn between her longing to stay near her father, as he fought what might be his last fight, and her need to be with Joshua when he returned Baby Sally to her mother.

Nell expressed her concern. "Bertie doesn't know you,

Joshua. If you come to her house with the baby, whoever is staying with her will call in all the men she can get, or shoot you herself, thinking you're the kidnapper. Bethany has to be with you when you take her back."

Reluctantly, Joshua agreed. They went back into the other room where the sound of Ben's harsh breathing seemed to beat against the log walls. Joshua and Nell sat before the fire to give Bethany a period of time alone beside her father.

Watching him struggle for every breath, Bethany deliberately refused to let herself give in to tears. Instead, she concentrated on joining the almost tangible feeling of prayer in the room. A glance at Nell and Joshua told her that each was lost in fervent, though silent, prayer.

After a time, as light dimmed in the cabin, she reluctantly dropped her father's limp hand and stood up. Nell changed the poultice on his chest then took the chair by his bed as Bethany and Joshua lit the lantern and prepared to go down to the church.

They decided not to stop to see Bertie on the way.

"We don't want to get up the hopes of the poor woman 'til we have the babe in our hands to give to her," Joshua said.

There was little activity in the valley as they rode down toward the church, Bethany on Rainbow leading the way and carrying the lantern. Not one of the cabins they could see from the road even showed any light.

"Usually you can see a little glow from the fireplace at least," Bethany murmured to herself. She looked back at Joshua, barely visible, following her on Chief. She decided not to share her strange feeling of uneasiness with him. After all, it was probably just the extraordinary excursion that caused it.

This time they rode down the lane from the road to the church. They dismounted in front of the church and dropped the horses' reins, allowing them to browse. Bethany turned their heads away from the cemetery to the other side of the church and the horses, possibly keeping a memory of being tethered there during church services, quietly moved off.

As they walked to the church door, Joshua took the lantern from Bethany. The door seemed to have a squeak when Joshua opened it that Bethany didn't remember hearing before. Almost unconsciously, she reached out toward Joshua to find his hand waiting for hers. They stood close together looking for Baby Sally in the flickering light of the lantern.

Still holding hands, they walked slowly down the aisle, looking on and under each bench. There was no sign of the baby. Bethany felt tears of disappointment stinging her eyes. Mattie was getting whatever satisfaction she derived from hurting people now. She must be laughing to herself up on the mountain. She may have even been lying about knowing where the baby was. There was no hope any longer that it hadn't been carried off by some wild animal or perhaps an even wilder human.

Then they heard a sound from behind the pulpit—a tiny mewing of a waking baby. Quickly it escalated into a lusty cry.

Bethany reacted like a mother. Dropping Joshua's hand, she hurried behind the pulpit ahead of him. Baby Sally was lying in a small homemade cradle wrapped in a clean crocheted shawl. Bethany wondered briefly if it might be the cradle and shawl that Mattie's own mother had nestled her in so long ago. A bottle of a substance that looked and smelled like goat's milk with a piece of leather twisted into a nipple was in the cradle beside her.

Bethany gathered the crying baby up into her arms. She smiled up at Joshua, who had rested the lantern on the floor beside them. "She looks like she's had good care. She's too loud to have been weakened."

Laughing, she pushed the leather nipple into the wide open mouth. A splash of milk spilled out over the baby's face and Bethany found a clean rag in the cradle to wipe it off. Then she carefully tipped the bottle just enough to let the milk dribble into the baby's mouth.

"Mattie used some creative thinking," Joshua said, pointing to the leather nipple. "Surely, we can get her to use her mind for better things than fooling people with pretense."

Bethany nodded. "But for now, we get to take Baby Sally back to her mother, and tell all the valley that she's home. Just as soon as she gets all this milk inside her greedy self." She pulled the baby more snugly against herself, just to say to her that she didn't mean it.

"It looks like someone has already told them," Joshua said. "There are lights coming down the lane."

Bethany raised her gaze from the baby's face to look out the open door. "And listen to them," she said. "They're celebrating already. And there are more lights coming across the cemetery."

"Give me the baby and stand behind me," Joshua said, with a new strain in his voice. "I've heard those sounds too many times before. They aren't sounds of celebration. They're sounds of an angry mob."

twelve

Joshua took the baby and pushed Bethany behind himself, with a wide sweep of his free arm. Even Bethany could recognize now that the noise of the approaching group was angry rather than exulting. But once they saw that Baby was there and healthy, surely they would turn to celebrating.

The leaders of the mob were at the open door. There was a short struggle there as several of the men tried to be the first to enter. Then one tall man pushed ahead and strode up to stand in front of the pulpit. Bethany felt her hands tremble as she recognized Dave Bradley.

He lifted up a lantern to shine full on Joshua. "Here he is, boys, just like Mattie told us. Come on in. Surround the bushwhacker, so he can't get away with the baby again."

The church filled up with shouting, angry men.

"Bushwhacker."

"Look, he's got the baby. He can't pretend he didn't take her."

"You'll never steal one of our children again."

"Get him, boys. We'll string him up."

"Let us get the baby first." An unidentified female scream came from outside the church door. It was followed by a cacophony of sounds made by women unable to push inside the church.

With a wave of heartsick emotion, Bethany realized that Mattie had achieved whatever revenge she was searching for at Joshua's expense. He was going to be killed by these normally kind people, goaded into a brawling mob by the bushwhackers' raid and the kidnapping of Bertie's baby. Mattie's evil meddling was doing just what she wanted it to do. Nell's belief that any stranger would be accepted in the valley in this intense period was naive.

But, even as she reacted to the angry sounds of the mob, Bethany was aware of the steady stance of Joshua in front of her. He stood, quietly cradling Baby Sally in his left arm and looking back at the jostling mass, making no attempt to respond to them.

His attitude calmed her a little. Perhaps if she really showed herself to them it might help to quiet these neighbors of hers. Before Joshua could stop her, she stepped out from behind him into the circle of lantern light.

"Please, neighbors, listen to me. This man isn't a bushwhacker. He hasn't hurt us. He didn't take the baby. Mattie. . ."

She was drowned out by angry voices, arguing among themselves.

"Look who's with him. Somebody rescue her." It was a woman's voice.

"Don't seem like she's looking for rescuing to me."

"But she's been taking care of us since Doc's been gone."

"Sure, Doc left us to go doctor them Yankees our boys are fighting and dying from on the battlefield."

Bethany recognized the shouter as Carl Dietz, whose son had been killed in the Confederate Army at the battle of Shiloh Church. She searched the crowd for the face of his wife. Sophie Dietz had been almost hysterical for days after the news came. Bethany saw her now far in the back, not taking part in the quarrels.

"No, he's been. . ." Again she was drowned out and she felt Joshua's quieting hand on her back.

"And why not when the Union men are fighting to keep our country together?" another voice called.

Bethany could see a slow shifting of men to each side of the crowded church as they let themselves get caught up in the seething current of passion that raged through the valley.

Joshua's hand left her back. To Bethany's surprise, she saw it raised toward the jostling, shouting crowd. His voice cut across the angry sounds with the unmistakable tones of ministry.

"May the peace of our Blessed Savior, Jesus, enter into your hearts."

The mob fell silent and turned in surprise to face Joshua. The benediction that they hadn't heard for so long brought the quieting reaction they would have given their minister back in those peaceful days when they tilled the land and went to church on Sunday.

There was a moment of stillness that could almost be touched. The hands which were raised against each other fell to their sides, while the seething sounds of shuffling feet suddenly stopped. The mouths which had opened to shout angry words, remained open in awe.

Then, shattering the silence, the baby suddenly wriggled in Joshua's arm and cried. The crowd seemed as one to remember why they were there.

"Blasphemy. Blasphemy. He's using preacher words to keep us from stringing him up." Bethany recognized Mattie's voice. She longed to face her and ask her why she had repaid their kindness with such evil behavior. Was it resistance to accepting help that her spirit needed and wanted?

Bethany remembered that Joshua had spoken sympathetically of her need as they rode down the mountain. But what was he thinking of her now that she had caused his life to be threatened? How could he continue trusting God and loving his fellow man when the very acts of serving Him caused such violence to himself?

Joshua stood quietly. Then, again, his hand rose over the throng and he repeated the blessing of peace. There was another moment of quiet in the church as the confused crowd tried to make sense of his actions.

This time he took advantage of it. "Friends and neighbors, we are in the church of our Savior. Will you desecrate it with hatred and threats of killing? Or will we be still and know that God still reigns?"

A woman's voice called out from just inside the door. "He's right, whoever he is. It's been so long since we've had church here, we've forgotten what this house is for."

Once again, Joshua took advantage of the momentary silence. "You all know Bethany Andrews. You know she's never done anything but good for you. Will you listen to her now?"

Bethany felt his hand on her back again. She breathed a quick prayer to God to put the right words in her mouth to help Joshua quiet this crowd.

Standing beside the pulpit, she knew that she couldn't ask God for help then try to mislead the crowd. She took in a deep breath.

"Friends, when the bushwhackers went through our valley, they left a man they hated because of his preaching for peace in our country. They beat him so badly he was unconscious, and they left him where they thought you would find him and kill him, if he didn't die from their beating. Instead Willie Bowers and I found him and secretly brought him here. When he regained consciousness. . ."

She paused, then decided not to talk about his memory loss. So far she was holding the attention of the crowd, but they weren't in any mood for long explanations.

". . .he told Nell and me the truth that he is a minister of the gospel. The bushwhackers hated him because he rode circuit, preaching peace. You just heard the only proof we need that it is true."

There was a long drawn-out murmur from the crowd, then

a strident voice calling out, "He didn't prove it to me and he's still got the baby."

Bethany felt her body tense. It was Dave Bradley again. She saw him trying to push his way through the crowd, which had shoved him back in their conflict.

"How do we know he's not holding Bethany against her will, too? Would she take the side of a stranger against us? Bethany, don't be afraid. We'll get you away from him."

"Big talk for someone who hides back in the mountains when the recruiters come through," Annie Bowers called. "My boy, Willie, who just this week went out to get in this war, would make two of you."

"Sure. Snuck out to fight with the Yankees against my son and all our boys who're trying to protect our ways." Bethany again recognized the bent figure of Carl Dietz.

"And why not fight for the Union? It's your boy who's rebelling against our own country. And your side that left my boy's body in some cold grave where I may never even get to bury it out in our graveyard with his mama and his granddaddy and grandmama, and he'll never come back to be a daddy to that baby up there." This time it was Clyde MacMillan, Jasper MacMillan's widowed father.

"The shape that graveyard's in, who'd want to be buried there?" Bethany didn't recognize the voice of the woman who was calling from just outside the door.

"Well, I happen to know that your own boy is riding with the bushwhackers," another female voice called. "Who scared our preacher out of the valley in the first place? Who's taking our animals and everything we raise to eat when they raid us?"

A scuffle broke out in the back of the church. *Oh,* Bethany thought, *will we never come together enough even to hear the healing words of a minister after being without one for so long?*

While Joshua stood quietly and Bethany watched in despair,

Tabitha Ballard suddenly forced her big body between the elderly men in the shoving match. "Shut up all of you. This is still a church. And that's our friend, Bethany, up there."

"Yes. Hush. Let her talk," several female voices called. Someone helped Tabitha pull the two men apart and they quieted down. There was the sound of many feet shifting, and light and shadows flicked about the room as men moved their lanterns.

Quickly, Bethany went on. "We went up to the mountain to treat a sore on Mattie's leg. To repay us, she told us that if we would come here tonight we would find the baby. As you can see, we did. I don't know why Mattie chose to send you all down here ready to kill Joshua Holt, the only preacher we've had in Falling Water Valley for more than a year, but she did. . ."

"She's lying. I deevined where the baby was," Mattie called out, pushing her way up the crowded aisle. "She never treated my leg. I ain't got a sore on my leg. He's a bushwhacker, come to kill our babies. I deevined it."

Joshua handed the baby to Bethany and stepped down to meet her. "Mattie, for love of Jesus, I forgive you and offer you His peace. But you will tell these people the truth. You will not lie to them anymore."

There was total stillness in the church as the two stood stiffly, their eyes locked in a silent struggle to prevail. Then, suddenly, Mattie turned and tried to run out of the church on her sore leg. The people in the aisle pressed against each other to make a path for her.

"It's true. She's limping," someone called. The words seemed to bring the crowd to life and there was a cacophony of asides to each other.

"Let's go after her."

"She's a witch."

"Let not a witch live."

The group turned their anger on Mattie as easily as it had erupted against Joshua a short time ago.

Joshua stepped back up behind the pulpit. "No, my friends. I know that you have been badly used and that the war has brought out anger and frustration and yearning to go back to the peaceful days of Falling Water Valley. But there has been enough hatred. Vengeance is mine, saith the Lord."

The movement in the church stopped, as they waited to see what was to come. "Now, Bethany has more to tell you."

There was another commotion at the door. Bertie burst through the cleared space left by Mattie. The listless woman who huddled by a fire kept going by other people had changed to a charging bear of a mother.

"Virgie told me my baby is here," she yelled. "I ran all the way down." She stopped as the baby in Bethany's arms roused up and started to cry again. "Oh, thank You, Jesus," she cried, raising her arms to heaven. "I promise to raise her to serve You." Then she hurried up to meet Bethany, who carried the baby to her. "Just let me hold her. Just let me hold her."

Smiling happily, Bethany handed the baby, wrapped in the shawl, to her. Bertie sank onto the front bench. She clutched the baby close to her chest and rocked her, crooning a wordless song of love. Then, without stopping her comforting humming, she unwrapped her and began searching her body for injury.

"As you can see, Mattie has taken good care of her," Bethany said. Then she stepped back beside Joshua and turned to the crowd. "I want to tell you that my father is home." A scattering of applause broke out. "But he is sick with pneumonia in our cabin. Nell is nursing him there. We need your prayers."

"We will. We'll pray for him, Bethany," someone called.

"Now perhaps it is time for you to go to your homes," Joshua said.

Tabitha stepped forward. "No, Preacher, no. We've missed a Sunday preaching for months. It's not Sunday but we're here now. Let's have a preaching out of you."

thirteen

There was a general murmur of assent. Without further words, the men sat on their side of the church and the women standing about the door filed in and found seats on the women's side, just as they had done all their lives. Someone brought up a lantern and set it beside Bethany's on the pulpit. Bethany slipped onto the bench beside Bertie, who had rewrapped Baby Sally and was cuddling the now quiet infant against her shoulder.

For this once, Bethany ignored the remembered injunction to look forward toward the minister, though that was all she wanted to do. She leaned against the end of the bench and watched the crowd for signs of danger to Joshua, in between proud glances toward him.

Joshua stood quietly at the pulpit, looking down on them as they settled down. Then he spoke to them.

"Be at peace among yourselves. See that none render evil for evil unto any man; but ever follow that which is good, both among yourselves and to all men." (I Thessalonians 5: 13, 15)

"You are good people, all of you. Some of you believe in the cause of the North and some in the cause of the South. What you believe, you believe in your hearts to be right, and I can't tell you differently. But you have lived side by side with your neighbors in Falling Water Valley for years before this sad war came between you. I ask you now, in the love of Christ, to give each other some forgiveness, and try to get back the spirit of community that made it possible for your ancestors who first settled here to survive. A spirit which has made your life here sweet as you helped each other over the bad times and celebrated the good ones. It's a spirit of love and neighborliness and we are told in the Bible to love our neighbor as ourselves."

Some of the warring neighbors turned to look at each other as if remembering days when they hunted and farmed in cooperation. But Bethany didn't see them shaking hands.

"Jesus loves each and every one of you," Joshua went on. "He doesn't love only Southerners or Northerners. He loves you as persons. I believe that we have made His heart glad when he looks down on Mrs. MacMillan holding her baby in the arms where she belongs. But I believe we break that heart with our hatred and anger against each other."

Bethany felt tears in her eyes as she watched the faces react in the dim light. She even saw tears running unchecked down the cheeks of some of them. Joshua spoke to them more about God's love and care for them. He asked them to try to forgive their neighbors and reminded them that they had worked together in trying to find the baby.

Then he led them in a prayer of thankfulness that the recent raid hadn't caused any deaths and for the return of Baby Sally and supplication for the recovery of Ben Andrews.

Under his hand of peace, they filed quietly out of the church. If some of the people were still not looking into each other's eyes or shaking hands, they were, at least for this night, not glaring at each other.

Bertie was the last to leave. She pressed Bethany's hand while holding her baby tightly to her chest. Joshua gathered the three of them into one big bear hug.

Joshua helped Bertie get on Chief with some difficulty since she refused to let Bethany have the baby while she mounted. Then he carried the lantern and walked beside the horses up to

Bertie's cabin. They made sure that Tabitha and Virgie were there ready to help with Baby Sally. The two women pressed gratitude and praise on Joshua, then Bethany and Joshua went back to the horses.

Joshua blew out the lantern. "We need to preserve our resources," he said. He didn't mount Chief but hooked the reins over his arm and walked beside him. Without asking herself why, Bethany did the same with Rainbow.

She strained, uselessly, to see him on the dark road. "You preached a good sermon tonight, Pastor," she said into the blackness. "The people of the valley will remember you with thankfulness."

Only the noises of the horses hoofs answered her. "Joshua?" she called. "You didn't blow out the lantern just to preserve our resources, did you?"

"Forgive me, Bethany. I suppose God is now looking at me like a sulky child. I should rejoice for every bit of progress we make against the hatred that covers the country, but instead I want Him to reward my tiniest effort by showering us with sudden peace. I know that we have to work harder for it, but I grieve that, though nobody walked out during the sermon, neither did they shake hands when it was over."

Bethany could only nod, even knowing that he couldn't see her. A sharp voice inside prodded her. *So, this is what it would be like. . .sharing the life of a dedicated minister at this time.*

She was glad to see the light of her cabin in front of them. They unharnessed the horses in the dark and let them find their way into their stable. Bethany turned to go into the cabin, but Joshua caught her hand and stopped her.

"Pray with me, Bethany."

She let her hand be buried in his while he thanked God for the events of the night, then asked forgiveness for his insufficient thankfulness. After the prayer, they stood silently for awhile. Bethany felt so close to God and to Joshua that there was no question in her mind that this was a special moment for them both.

The inside voice was softer. *This, too, would be a part of sharing a life with someone like Joshua.*

Yet, had anyone asked her to be thinking of a shared life?

❧

Nell met them at the door of the cabin, a huge smile on her face. "It's passed. The climax passed and his fever's broken," she said. "He's sleeping now." She had extravagantly lit candles all about the room in celebration. They augmented the light of the fireplace until the room was almost bright.

Bethany threw her arms around her and the three of them held hands and bowed their heads in a prayer of thanksgiving for Ben's improvement. Then Bethany told Nell about the happenings at the church.

"We may not be able to get the church open again 'til the war is over, but we had one good service tonight," she said happily. The gloom of the last part of their trip home was gone completely for her. She hoped that it was for Joshua.

Nell looked at Joshua. "We thank you," she said simply.

"Doing God's work is my life," he answered just as simply. "I know that for sure now. But I couldn't have managed the crowd without Bethany."

"Do you have a helpmate?" Nell carefully didn't look at Bethany when she innocently asked the question.

Joshua hesitated, looking troubled, and Bethany caught her breath.

"I don't think I could ask a woman to live the life I would give her. . .a life of waiting and loneliness while I move about from place to place," he answered seriously.

Bethany strove to control her expression. Was he telling her that no woman could compete with his dedication to his calling? A dedication that caused him to give up a home and even risk and accept physical injury. The story of the apostle Paul came to her mind, and she reminded herself again of the brevity of their acquaintance.

But so much had happened it seemed like forever. She didn't try to meet his eyes or know if he was looking at her.

Ben woke then, racked by coughing, and they all went to his bedside. Nell helped him hold a pillow to his chest while he painfully brought up the thick material that had been choking off his breathing.

"We thank God for every bit of it that you expel," Nell said in the practical prayer of the healer. Ben nodded and managed a weak smile before he sank back onto the bed and drifted off again.

"While he's sleeping, we'll eat whatever meal it may be time for," Nell said, looking at the clock on the mantel. "It seems to have stopped," she added.

"It does that when it doesn't get wound," Bethany answered drily. "But I believe Joshua and I ate our supper before we went down to the church. You eat now and sleep a bit. I'll stay with Daddy. I'm too excited to sleep anyway."

"I'll stay with you," Joshua said.

Bethany struggled briefly with her emotions then nodded her acceptance. She blew out all the candles except one on the cherrywood table. Joshua pulled another chair beside the bed from the table and they sat without talking for awhile. Bethany let a feeling of contentment flood over her.

"Who are you? You look familiar."

They both looked at Ben. He was looking at Joshua, his face free of the pain that had been there since he first came to them in the church.

"This is Joshua Holt, Daddy. You told us at the church that you'd heard him preach. And he held you on Chief when we brought you up from the church. Don't you remember?"

Ben shook his head. "The last thing I remember is relief at

seeing Chief and Rainbow down at the church," he said. "How many days have I lost?"

"Only one, Daddy." Bethany was surprised herself that so much had happened in so short a time. "But it was a long one," she added. "Now, since you're awake, I'll get some beef broth. Nell will have my scalp if I don't feed you every time I have a chance."

But Ben wanted to talk. Bethany kept him opening his mouth for broth by going into more detail about who Joshua was and how he happened to be there. Then she had to hold the spoon while he told them his own story.

"When I left here I went with the Confederates," he said, seeming to forget that she knew where he was going when he left.

"I know, Daddy. I got your letter just a few days ago."

"One of my letters," Ben said. "I wrote you every chance I could get. I was needed so badly. I did my best for the Confederate boys."

"I treat all who are brought to me for we are all children of God," Bethany murmured. "I've used the thought behind those words several times already."

She remembered that those words had helped her decide to stop and help Joshua, even while thinking that he was a bush-whacker. She glanced at him and found him looking at her as though he understood.

Ben opened his mouth for another spoonful of broth and swallowed it slowly.

"A few Confederates ran into some Union men. It was just a surprise skirmish. We hadn't set up a hospital area yet, so I went out on the battlefield where several men had been wounded. The Union overran us and we were all taken prisoner."

Another paroxysm of coughing interrupted him. Bethany reached across him and got the pillow for him to hold against his chest.

"Daddy, shouldn't you stop talking now? We can find out the rest later." She agonized with every painful spasm that he struggled with. The knowledge that he had been held prisoner brought tears to her eyes. What kind of treatment had he received?

At the end of the coughing spell, he drifted off to sleep, the pillow still clutched to his chest. Bethany tried to scrub at the tears in her eyes as best she could with the spoon in one hand and the bowl in the other. She felt a clean cloth wiping her eyes gently. Joshua placed the cloth back into the pocket of his borrowed trousers and laid his hand over hers.

"Just remember that he is safely here," he whispered.

"They took us to Illinois," her father suddenly continued, probably unaware that he had slept, "then when they discovered that I'm a doctor they released me. It seems that neither side is holding doctors prisoner. They gave me a horse and I started home, shaking with ague. Someone stopped me somewhere in Tennessee, or maybe Kentucky, and took my horse. I walked the rest of the way."

Bethany let the spoon drop into the bowl of broth while she bowed her head to hide the tears she felt gushing from her eyes as she thought again of her father, sick and exhausted, trying to get to them.

Joshua gently took the bowl from her hand and when she could see through the tears, she saw him carefully feeding the rest of the broth to Ben. Then he took the bowl to the table and came back to his chair.

Ben slipped back into sleep, exhausted by the interval of eating and talking. Bethany shifted the quilts to cover an exposed arm. She kept her face turned away from Joshua, unwilling to let him see the tears that were still there.

He took both her hands in his. He didn't force her to look up but quietly kept her hands in the warmth of his, sending a steady comfort to her.

Then he released one hand to pull her head gently against his shoulder. For a minute she resisted, then she gave way to her fatigue and emotion and let herself relax against him. He shifted his body slightly and brought his arm about her shoulders. Without words, remembering their moments in prayer together at the stable, Bethany felt closer to him than she had ever felt to anyone, even her father.

In the lovely feeling of lassitude and comfort, she drifted off to sleep.

The sounds of Nell stirring up the fire woke her.

Nell walked across the room. She seemed not to see Bethany's position against Joshua's shoulder, but her brilliant smile displayed her approval of everything in the room.

"Ben's forehead is dry and cool," she whispered. "Look how easy he's breathing. And how relaxed he is."

"That's more than a couple of other people are." Joshua stood up with a low groan as Bethany quickly moved from his shoulder. He stretched and massaged his muscular shoulders, then gently rubbed the area of the bruise on his chest. Then he grinned at Bethany. "However, don't ever think you have a heavy head," he quipped.

Bethany tried to think of a light remark to cover her confusion then, seeing the gentle tenderness in his eyes, realized that she didn't need to feel apologetic. Something had changed in their relationship. Something that didn't need words. Not at this time anyway.

She smiled back. "Did you sleep?" she asked.

"Some," he answered. "Some I spent thinking about the events of the past few days and thanking God for the nasty beating I received."

Nell made a noise that wasn't quite her usual snort. "That reminds me, I'll need to dress your cuts and bruises after you eat. Maybe we can take that brace off your chest. Your face is almost looking better." Then she looked soberly at him for a moment. "I don't quite understand that last remark you made. Are you saying God made those men beat you into unconsciousness?"

"I don't pretend to always know the mind of God," Joshua answered, "but I can see how He can use the actions of evil men to bring good."

"Then explain this war, Pastor. Explain the spite that's tearing this valley apart. That's going to last 'til we're all dead."

They all turned to look at Ben. He was awake, watching and listening to them.

Joshua answered him seriously, "I don't think I can," he admitted. "It does appear that war is the only way we can throw out the evil of slavery that's hurting the masters as well as the slaves. And this week the people of the valley have shown that at least some Union and Confederate sympathizers can work together to find a baby. Maybe they can come together as neighbors again afterwards."

Ben nodded, though his expression showed some confusion about some of Joshua's references. Still, Bethany knew that he appreciated Joshua's candid admission that he didn't have all the answers.

"And, Daddy, Joshua turned a riot into a church service last night," she said. Then, sometimes all talking at once, sometimes taking turns, they filled Ben in on all the recent happenings in the valley.

fourteen

"Just the same, I'm going up to see about Mattie this morning," Bethany said.

She and Joshua sat at the table eating bowls of hot oatmeal sweetened with honey while Ben, propped against a blanket and pillow in his bed, slowly spooned up a thinned gruel of the same thing. Nell had attempted to feed him but he insisted that he was no longer a baby. So she sat beside the bed beaming at him.

Now she jerked around to stare at Bethany. "After what she tried to do last night?"

"I need to check on her. . .to check that leg and that she's all right," Bethany said stubbornly.

Joshua nodded. "I'll go with you," he said.

Though both Nell and Ben continued to express doubts about the trip, Bethany was determined and Joshua understood. They only waited for Nell to take him into her office and doctor his cuts, after which she pronounced him to be a fast healer. Bethany, thinking of all they had done since he woke up in the church, felt grateful that none of it had damaged his body further.

Before they went up the mountain, they stopped at Bertie's cabin. They found her rocking the baby.

"I haven't put her down since I got her back," she said.

"She hasn't stopped grinning, either," said Tabitha Ballard, who had spent the night with them in case the baby should need something.

"I can't. . .I don't know the words. . .to thank you," whispered Bertie, looking from Joshua to Bethany.

Joshua responded with a brief prayer, directing her thanks to God, and asking for health and peace for the mother and baby. Then they left the cabin.

"We aren't going to find that kind of happiness up on the mountain," Bethany said, as they turned their horses' heads upward.

"Whatever we find, Bethany, with the help of God we can handle it," Joshua answered tranquilly. "Let's just enjoy the scenery and the good-tasting air for now."

They rode in silence for awhile, Bethany trying to absorb some of Joshua's composure, and thanking God with all her heart that he delighted in the beauty of nature as much as she did. She smiled to herself, happy that they could take pleasure in each other's company without having to fill every minute with sound.

He turned and looked at her. "Why are you smiling?" he asked gently.

Bethany attempted to think of something to cover her confusion, then she realized that she didn't need to. She could just answer honestly.

"I was just thinking that you don't meet many people you can share a comfortable silence with," she said.

"It's been said that this is the measure of the ability of two people to really be friends," he answered, guiding Chief around a fallen log. "But, Bethany, I know that I had already formed a deep friendship with you when I really woke up down in the church. And not just because you stopped to help me when you could have passed on by. I didn't even know that then. Though it's good to know that you did the Christian thing, just as you are doing with Mattie."

Bethany let Rainbow find her own way around the log and come back to the trail before she answered. "Sometimes it's hard to hold onto the feeling that I did the right thing. Oh, not that I'm sorry we helped you," she added hastily, coming up beside him and seeing his surprised expression.

"But Willie didn't want to stop when we were on the way to treat people wounded by the bushwhackers. And I forced him to, and then to keep you a secret. . .I know he wanted to tell everyone and go down and finish you off. . .he was so sure that you were one of the men who'd raided the valley. . ."

"Wait a minute." Joshua stopped Chief and reached out a hand to Rainbow's bridle. "You're confusing me completely. Tell me about Willie. Is he a beau?" His expression was hard to read.

"Oh, no. He's a fifteen-year-old neighbor. We had a routine that he'd take me down to the schoolhouse when we were raided and Nell would stay at the cabin to treat anyone who was hurt near there."

Joshua looked relieved, but he didn't start the horses up. "Bethany, I know I have no right to ask, but, is there anyone who is a beau? But, then, of course there must be. You're a beautiful young woman."

"Thank you, and no." Bethany was silent for a moment, then, again wanting to be totally honest, she added, "Well, there's Dave Bradley, who sometimes pretends that we're interested in each other, but we're not really. He was in the church last night. But he's not important."

Joshua gave an exaggerated sigh of relief and they both laughed. Then he became serious.

"Tell me why you have doubts about this neighbor boy. Is it because he is becoming so used to fighting and people hurting each other and not caring that he doesn't react the way you want him to?"

"No. Well, it's true that he's seen too much of that, but now he's going to see even more. What happened is, he ran away to join the Union Army and I think that I pushed him to go sooner than he would have because I forced him to help you and not tell his father about it."

"And if he should be hurt or killed you may feel responsible."

Bethany nodded, glad that Joshua understood so quickly. Then she felt a flash of resentment when he started Chief up again and went off ahead of her without offering any solace. She sat dumbfounded on Rainbow, who followed Chief without any direction from her. They went single file through a rough portion of the trail without talking.

After they went around a large rock and came to a wider area, Joshua pulled Chief around to face her so abruptly that Rainbow almost bumped them. Bethany jerked back on the reins.

"Bethany, do you know how hard it is to try to preach the love of God to men who honestly think that learning to hate their spiritual brothers, sometimes their physical brothers and cousins and neighbors, enough to be able to kill them, is good? Can you imagine how I can talk of universal love to the mother of two sons who are away fighting each other? I wish I had the answers. I wish I could say the right words to make your neighbors in Falling Water Valley go down to that church every Sunday from now on, but you know they won't. I wish I could promise you that Willie won't be hurt or killed, but I can't. But I can remind you that, in His story of the Good Samaritan, our Lord told us to stop and help the wounded stranger. And I believe that, after this war is over, many men and women will carry memories of living by the grace of helpful strangers."

Bethany couldn't answer for the tears in her throat, but she nodded and didn't try to hide the tears on her cheeks from him. He turned Chief back toward the mountaintop and they didn't try to talk before coming out onto Mattie's clearing.

They didn't see Mattie. The hut had an air of desertion about it.

"Maybe because I've always found her sitting out in front.

Bethany didn't realize that she'd spoken her thought aloud 'til Joshua answered her. "Let's hope we find her all right inside."

They dismounted and dropped their horse's reins. Joshua put his hand on her arm as they mounted the rock that Mattie used as her front step. He positioned her behind himself and entered the cabin first.

It was empty. An eerie silence hung over the place, intensified by a dampness drifting from the rock which made up the back wall. Joshua knelt and stirred the ashes of her fire with a finger.

"Cold," he said. "She probably didn't spend the night here. It wasn't so cold that she would have to have a fire, but it was chilly."

"Where do you suppose she is?" Bethany asked.

"Maybe wherever she was keeping the baby," Joshua answered practically. "You said you didn't see any signs of the baby here the first time you came up and, of course, we didn't when we were here yesterday."

"I suppose there's no chance of finding her hideout. I really do want to check on that leg. It could get very bad."

"I don't see how we can find her, Bethany. There's probably dozens of small caves and holes on this mountain, or she may have another hut somewhere back in the trees. I think we may have to wait and see if she'll care enough about herself to come down to you."

Silently, Bethany agreed and they mounted their horses and started back down. About halfway down, Joshua stopped Chief and reached out for Rainbow's reins.

"Let's not go down yet. I want some time for just the two of us. Can you show me the waterfall that the valley is named after?"

Bethany nodded. "It's just a small one. But it's pretty. Rainbow and I come up to see it once in awhile. But," she warned, "it's not on a trail and it's pretty rugged." She grinned. "Nell doesn't know we come up alone. She'd fuss that a bear or something would get me."

Joshua grinned and Bethany's heart speeded up. "Lead Chief and me to it," he said.

Laughing for no reason, Bethany turned Rainbow off the trail, guiding her through the trees in the general direction of the waterfall. Soon they came out into a place where tiny rocks deposited over the years by high water made a small bow of pebble beach beside the stream.

Rivulets of water spilled across a jutting rock half again taller than a man's head, sending mists into the cool air. They pulled their horses up, side by side.

"It was bigger the last time I was here," Bethany said ruefully. "I guess it dries up some in autumn."

"Don't apologize for it. A little waterfall has its place, too," Joshua said. "Let's get off the horses. There's something I want to do."

Joshua dismounted beside her and reached up to catch her as she slipped off Rainbow. The horses made a kind of private enclosure for them as Joshua, instead of letting her go, turned her to face him, keeping his arms around her.

He held her for a long moment, looking deeply into her eyes. Then he bent and touched his lips to hers, gently at first, then slowly deepening, until Bethany felt that her very spirit was flowing into his as she let her own arms wrap themselves around him.

But she pulled back first.

"Was that what you wanted to do?" she asked shakily.

"It's what I've wanted to do since the first time I saw your face shimmering through the haze around my eyes back in the church," he said seriously. "I've been repeating to myself what I told Nell yesterday about not asking a woman to share my life, but I don't seem to be listening to myself. Bethany, I know it's too soon to ask you if you're willing to live that life. . ."

He placed two fingers on her lips when she tried to speak, but she knew that her eyes were giving him the answer to the question he wouldn't yet ask. An answer that she knew would be yes, whenever he chose to hear it.

They stood silently holding each other until the horses, apparently thinking that humans didn't know how to act, moved away from them.

"Now, let's go look at that waterfall." Joshua dropped his arms from around her and took her hand, leading her across the gravel. Bethany let him change the subject for now.

They stood close enough to the waterfall for tiny cool beads of water to dampen their faces. Bethany savored the deep bond that shimmered between them. No matter what happened, she would never feel mist in her face again without thinking of the warmth of her hand in Joshua's and the touch of his lips on hers.

"Look," Joshua said suddenly, "there's a little low ledge where we could walk behind the waterfall. I'll bet we can see rainbows. Let's do it."

"Let's," Bethany agreed. Laughing and still holding hands, they slipped behind the falling water.

"Be careful," Joshua said. "The rock is slick here. It wouldn't freeze us if we fell in, but it's pretty chilly."

Bethany stopped and rested her back against the rock. "Oh, Joshua, look at the trees through the water. It looks like they're waving to us. And it's true, there are little rainbows all over."

He watched with her for a minute, then said, "My other hand is feeling air coming out of a hole in this rock. I think there's a cave here. Do you suppose this is where the old pioneer hid from the Indians?"

"Probably," Bethany answered, not much interested. "But we can't go in," she added practically. "We don't have a light."

Joshua turned away from her, looking into the emptiness beside him. "There's a little glow coming from inside. I think it's a fire, Bethany."

fifteen

A small bleat came from the cave.

"Joshua, is that a goat?"

"It sounds like it. I think we may have found Mattie's hiding place for the baby, Bethany."

"You mean she carried that baby behind all this water? She could have given it pneumonia or. . ."

Joshua put his hand over her mouth. "It's a little late to be quiet," he whispered, "but she may be listening. Stay here. I'm going in."

Bethany shook her head. "Safety in numbers," she whispered back. "Hold my hand."

Knowing that they couldn't stay outside the cave arguing, Joshua gave in, glad that they were positioned so that he would go in first.

He stooped and quickly stepped inside and to the side of the entrance, tugging at Bethany's hand to pull her over beside him. He could feel her hand shaking in excitement or fear and pulled her against him as they stood waiting for their eyes to adjust to the dim light coming from a dying fire several feet from them.

The cave was larger than it had seemed from the outside. Though it was fairly narrow, it extended well into the rock. Air was coming out of the depths, telling them that there must be another opening somewhere in the back.

Slowly they started picking out separate objects in the cave, set far enough back to escape spray from the waterfall. A bed, that looked to be made from planks set on bricks and a real feather or cornhusk mattress.

Better, Joshua thought, *than the one in her hut on the mountain.*

There was a chair as well, an old rocker. "She must have rocked the baby," Bethany whispered.

Joshua squeezed her hand, hearing the catch of tears in her voice. They still hadn't located Mattie, who might or might not be in the cave somewhere. The repeated bleating of a goat, somewhere out of their sight, suggested that the cave might have branches leading back from the part they could see.

"We have to see about the goat at least," Bethany whispered. "If it's tied up it may be starving."

In answer, Joshua tugged on her hand again, and they walked carefully between the bed and the fire, seeing no indication that Mattie was there.

The goat was tied in a small offshoot of the main cave. There were bits of hay in front of it and water in a clay bowl.

"Mattie can't have been gone long," Joshua said in a low tone.

"Mattie ain't gone at all and she ain't going back with you. Those people down there ain't going to give me a fair trial for taking that sweet baby that Bertie was too mean and stupid to take care of. They'd just string me up." The voice came out of somewhere in the darkness in the back of the cave.

Bethany answered first, overcome with a momentary resentment at Mattie's response to their compassion for her. "But that's what you tried to get them to do to Joshua."

"I've got a gun on you," was the only answer from the darkness. "It's a good one that belonged to my pa. I can see you against the fire."

"Mattie, you will have to answer for taking the baby, but we came to see about your leg," Joshua called. "Why don't you come out and let Bethany clean it and put a new dressing on it?"

"Don't need you," Mattie called. "I changed it myself. It's better. They're looking for me all over the mountain, but you're the only ones who found my cave. I can't let you go back out and tell them. I'll have to kill you. I'm kind of sorry, Bethany. You've been good to me and all."

"Then let Bethany go," Joshua called. "I'll stay here in the cave with you till she has time to get word to the sheriff at Asheville to come down and protect you from the people of the valley."

Mattie answered with a harsh laugh. "Why you think I want to go to the jail in Asheville? Without being free to walk this mountain, I got no life."

"Mattie, you can't kill Bethany. She's the only one who ever showed you any kindness." He squeezed Bethany's hand lightly.

Was he trying to give her a signal? Bethany was concerned at the impatience in his voice. Surely he wasn't thinking of trying to rush Mattie. She clutched his hand tighter.

There was silence for awhile in the back of the cave. Then Mattie spoke, something that was almost laughter in her voice.

"All right, Preacher, I'll make a deal with you. You just pray to Jesus to deevine for you what kind of gun I've got back here. If you're right, I'll let you go and kill myself. If you're wrong, I'll shoot you one at a time."

"I won't offer such a prayer, Mattie, and I won't encourage you to kill yourself. But I will pray that you will accept the peace Jesus can bring you whether you're up here on the mountain or down in Asheville in jail."

Bethany sent a quick prayer of her own that she could face death as bravely as Joshua. She heard a rustle from the blackness where Mattie hid and felt herself being pushed violently away from Joshua. Through her confused sense of uncontrolled staggering she heard the grunt of the little goat as she crashed into it and fell.

For minutes none of the three moved. Then Bethany twisted away from the goat as she saw Mattie's bulk come into the dim glow of the fire. "Maybe you've got something I need, Preacher," she said. She threw a long barreled rifle down at his feet. The clang of metal against rock reverberated through the depths of the cave.

"Wasn't no powder in it anyway," Mattie said, kicking the gun away. "Haven't been able to get powder or lead since the war started. I've been living on rabbits and things I can catch in traps."

Her tone was as conversational as if they were standing in a parlor somewhere in the ordinary world. Bethany realized that she was holding her breath and let it out as silently as possible. She made no further attempt to move, though she was now becoming aware of the rank odor of the little goat which had stopped bleating and was busily investigating her hair.

Joshua looked at Mattie for a long moment, then he put his arm around her shoulder. Mattie suddenly slumped against him, sobbing.

"Mommie, Mommie," she cried. "You ain't hugged me for so long. Why were you gone so long, Mommie? Why didn't you help me when Pa hit me?"

"Joshua, she's. . ." Bethany scrambled to her feet. Mattie was rapidly descending into the mental abyss she had skirted for so long. She moved to Mattie's other side.

"We're going out of here now, Mattie. Just stay with us." Joshua's voice was calm and comforting.

Mattie allowed herself to be led from the cave. Only on the ledge behind the waterfall did she pull away and lead them out as if announcing that the retreat she had kept hidden for so long was still her territory.

She bunched herself into a withdrawn bundle of ragged

clothing that Joshua held on Chief's saddle while he rode behind her. He and Bethany said little as they went down the mountain. At the last minute, Bethany had untied the unhappy little goat. She held its tether as it ran briskly along beside Rainbow.

When they reached home, she tied it in the stable and gave it some of Rainbow's oats, hoping it liked them. It immediately chewed away contentedly.

She unharnessed the horses, then followed Joshua and Mattie into the house. They took Mattie into the combination treatment room/bedroom of Bethany's house to the consternation of Nell.

"I'm sorry, Nell," Bethany said. "But we don't want to take her into the room with Daddy."

"Goodness, Bethany, whatever are we going to do with her?" Nell asked, looking at her bed where they had let Mattie curl into an outsized ball. "And we'll have the whole valley in here once someone finds out she's here."

Joshua sighed. "I wish I could say that after my sermon last night, the people of the valley have decided not to seek revenge, but I'm afraid it hasn't happened. But we didn't see anyone on the way down. I think they've all gone home to rest awhile and get back to their work. I'll take her over to Asheville tonight. . ."

Bethany's breath suddenly hurt her chest. He would leave tonight.

". . .if you will let me borrow Chief," Joshua continued.

Bethany's chest eased. He was coming back. Though he had addressed Nell instead of her, she knew that he was aware of her emotions.

"Of course. Anything to get her where she can be watched and her shenanigans won't be stirring up uproars here in the valley," Nell said. Then she grinned. "I've been planning a long night's sleep in my bed in here tonight, now that Ben's so much better."

Impulsively, Bethany threw her arms around Nell. "Nell, thank you so much for the great care you've taken of Daddy. How can we ever repay you?"

"You don't need to repay me," Nell answered, returning Bethany's hug. "I've only done what pleasures me greatly."

Joshua, smiling down at them, indicated that he was going in to see Dr. Andrews. Bethany knew that it showed his sensitivity that he was leaving to give them a few minutes alone with their emotions.

He went into the other room. Bethany, suddenly feeling as if her legs couldn't hold her any longer, sank onto a rustic stool beside the treatment table.

"Bethany, I can't believe how much has happened in the past few days. It's like a whole new world has opened up here in the valley. And," Nell glanced over at Mattie, sleeping deeply on her bed, "whatever happens with Mattie, Falling Water Valley is going to be better off without her."

Bethany smiled. "Joshua's honesty and integrity in the cave made Mattie realize that he has something she needs. I can only believe that he'll finish the job of bringing her to Jesus, now that she knows that someone cares. I know she must have quiet and peace for her mind to heal, too. Nell, I'm going to ask Joshua to bring her back to live with me once she answers to the kidnapping charge in Asheville."

Nell shook her head. "Do you realize how hard that would be, considering how the valley people are feeling now?"

Bethany nodded. "I'm not fooling myself that it will be easy, but I feel like she is partly my responsibility since it was at my insistence that she let me treat her leg and that led to. . . all this."

"And," she felt a deeper color enter her cheeks but she plowed on, feeling a need to express the deep commitment that had entered her being with Joshua's kiss, "this will be the first of many undertakings I hope God will allow Joshua and me to accomplish together."

Nell reached over and hugged her. "Bethany, maybe it's just because I've got a few emotions running through my own mind, but I almost believe you can handle even Mattie. Now, I'm going to check on Baby Sally and remind everyone that, no matter how glad we are that Dr. Ben is back, no one is to visit or call on him for sickness 'til we say he's well enough. That way, too, we'll be sure they won't find Mattie before Joshua can get her out tonight."

Bethany smiled. "I told them last night that he's back, but I know they'll want to talk about it."

Nell had barely gone out the door when Joshua came in from the other room and stood in almost exactly the same place. He took both her hands in his, then moved his hands up to hold her shoulders firmly, pulling her up from the stool to face him.

Bethany closed her eyes, remembering their kiss up by the waterfall. She didn't even pretend to herself that she wasn't hoping he would repeat it.

sixteen

"Bethany, open your eyes," he said gently.

He looked down at her soberly. "Bethany, I must apologize to you for the kiss up on the mountain, so soon after getting to know you. I want you to understand that I meant no lack of respect for you. I simply let the many things that have happened make me forget. . .the circumstances. Please forgive me."

Bethany looked at him in distress. "You're sorry that you kissed me."

"Oh, Bethany, don't be hurt. I'm only sorry that I didn't wait until I had known you longer and had permission from your father to court you."

Bethany looked him full in the face. "Perhaps we don't have the time during this war to do things the way we usually do. And, perhaps because I grew up with my father mostly in the mountains, I didn't learn the wiles of women, so I won't pretend now. Joshua, I'm not sorry for the kiss."

Joshua let his hands slip from her shoulder down her arms to hold her hands closely in both of his.

"I appreciate and understand your honesty, Bethany, and it makes me happy. Just the same, I won't kiss you again 'til I come back from Asheville and get proper permission from your father."

"Then," said Bethany, smiling mischievously, "I suppose I must kiss you good-bye."

Standing on tiptoe, she placed her lips against his. He

cupped her head in both hands and returned the kiss gently. Then he released her and stepped back.

"That should keep us close 'til we can kiss hello." Bethany pulled her hand from his and placed it on his arm. "Now, I'm going to get some food for you," she said.

So far, Joshua, used to being alone, had waited on himself. Now she wanted to wait on him. She went into the other room and heated a feast of chicken and noodles that Nell had managed to put together earlier.

She carried his food to him, putting the same emotion into serving him, that she had felt in their kisses. The look accompanying his simple "Thank you" told her that he understood the gesture.

She brought in food for Mattie and herself. They woke Mattie. She seemed somewhat restored by the sleep and fiercely refused Bethany's offer to feed her. She cleaned the plate then announced to Joshua that she was ready to go with him to Asheville.

"Shouldn't you sleep first?" Bethany asked, admitting to herself that she was hoping for a little more time before Joshua left. But concerned, also, that his still healing body had been given very little sleep.

"I think we should get out of the valley before anyone finds out that Mattie is here," Joshua answered. "I'm sure that Chief knows the way out and we'll be safer in the dark. Once we're out of the valley we can make camp and travel the rest of the way in daylight, taking out time. We'll have to give Chief time to rest from the double load, but I can walk sometimes."

"Aren't you afraid that she. . .?" Bethany spoke in a low tone.

Joshua stopped her. "I've spent many nights in camp without sleeping. Since she's also used to being awake at odd hours, I hope to talk with her about her soul. I think she will not try to escape such grace as our Jesus Christ offers."

"She'll need a cape. I don't know where she left her deer-skin one. I'll lend her one of mine. It's only wool and it will be small for her but it should keep her warm enough."

He agreed. They said very little more to each other since Mattie was now hanging on every word. Bethany wondered if she may have been listening earlier while they thought she was asleep.

After they ate and it was fully dark, Joshua went in with Nell for a prayer with Ben while Bethany stayed with Mattie. Then he drew Mattie into a circle with Bethany and asked God's blessings on their trip and on Bethany's work while they were gone.

Bethany had to force herself to turn loose of his hand. She didn't try to hide the tears in her eyes as they went out to ride double on Chief.

❧

In spite of her sadness at Joshua's leaving, Bethany slept well on her pallet by the fire, enjoying the sound of her father's easy breathing when she did wake. Surprisingly, she didn't feel any anxiety about Joshua. "My Jesus, they are in Your hands," she whispered, and soon fell back into a deep sleep.

❧

"Bethany, Ben and I need to talk to you," Nell said, after Bethany had rolled up her pallet and they had finished their breakfast.

Bethany looked over at Ben and saw him sitting up against the pillows grinning at her. She looked back to Nell, who had moved to his side, and saw an answering smile on her face.

"Could I possibly guess what you want to talk to me about?" she asked mischievously.

"Now, Daughter, you must wait and let me make this announcement after properly preparing you to accept a new stepmother," Ben answered, without even trying to control his outrageous smile.

"As if I need preparation to accept Nell as my stepmother," Bethany chided, coming over to the bed and catching Nell's hand. "She's been like a mother and a dear friend rolled into one ever since you left."

Ben reached out a hand to each of them. "I'm only sorry that it took so long and so much pain before I realized that it was Nell who had kept me from wandering on, away from Falling Water Valley. Now she's helped me to finally heal, and I don't mean just physically. I thank God for her. I'm sorry, Bethany, that I carried you about with me while I wandered for so long."

He leaned back against the pillows, his still recovering body exhausted by the emotion and effort of such a long speech.

Bethany adjusted his pillows, then leaned forward and kissed him lightly on the forehead. "Don't be sorry, Daddy. I think you may have been preparing me for my mission in life."

The fact that neither of them questioned her meaning told her that the feelings that had so quickly built up between Joshua and her were no secrets from them. She kissed Nell just as lightly, then went into the other room to give them some time alone. As she closed the door, she saw Nell readjusting the pillows that she had just fixed behind her father, and grinned to herself.

❧

Joshua wasn't able to predict when he might be able to bring Chief back, but Bethany hoped it would be only a few days. However, it was two long weeks before Ben, who was out of bed and sitting by a window, announced that he could see Chief and another horse coming up the road. He was back sleeping in his own bedroom, while Nell had moved back to her own house, though she spent the daytime hours with them.

She had borrowed a horse from Tabitha and Nathan Ballard.

She was working with her herbs in Ben's room now, while he sat in the main room of the cabin with Bethany.

Bethany dropped the hen she was cutting up for soup on the table, barely catching it before it slid across the table and onto the floor. She hurried to the door and, ignoring the chill in the air, flung it open, ready to welcome Joshua.

As the two riders came closer, disappointment crashed down on her like a physical weight. She recognized Mattie on Chief but there was a strange young boy on the other horse. She turned away to hide her tears from her father.

The riders brought their horses close to the porch. The boy tied his horse to a tree, but Mattie dropped Chief's reins. The horse moved off toward his stable. Mattie, after looking in some confusion toward the open door of the cabin, followed him.

Bethany could see even as she moved off that someone had found a better, cleaner dress for her large body. She looked like any normal woman in the cape Bethany had lent her. Her thoughtfulness for Chief, and the possibility that she felt some uneasiness at seeing them again, told Bethany that she had undergone some changes while she was gone.

Meanwhile the boy came to the door. "I'm Jimmie Carson," he announced shyly. "Preacher sent me to bring Chief back."

Bethany moved back from the door. "Come in," she invited, trying to hide her disappointment that it was him and not Joshua. "Let me get you something to eat."

The boy removed his shapeless cap, leaving on his home-spun coat. He sat cautiously at the table.

"I brought a letter from Preacher," he said, pulling a wrinkled piece of paper from his britches' pocket. "I kept it here to be sure not to lose it," he said proudly.

Bethany turned from the fireplace where she was retrieving a potato baked in the ashes and moving the kettle of dandelion tea forward to heat. For a minute, she stood stiffly, dreading to read it. Joshua was going to tell her that he wasn't coming back to Falling Water Valley.

She turned back, slit the baked potato, and put it on a plate. She placed it in front of Jimmie before she could force herself to touch the letter.

Then she picked up the paper, not noticing Jimmie's look of surprise that she didn't give it to Ben, and slowly opened it.

My Dear Bethany,

God has opened up an opportunity that will keep me from returning to Falling Water Valley for some time. I have been asked to conduct a protracted meeting in a cove in Tennessee where there have been no church services for a long while. Perhaps the experience in your church helped me understand the deep need of the people.

However that may be, Bethany, this summons has reminded me of my long-held view that my calling to God's service leaves me in a position which would be severely unfair to a wife.

Perhaps it is better that I can't come back to the valley and you immediately, for it will give you time to reconsider any implied commitment to me. I know in my heart that you are not a flirt who kisses with abandon whoever is near. Bethany, I don't want to hurt you but consider carefully if you wish to continue to accept my courtship, for I must put my service to God before all else.

I'm sending Mattie back with Jimmy. She has come to Christ and found a great deal of comfort from Him and has expressed a desire to return and try to undo the harm she has done in the valley. I know that you will help her in her endeavors.

*The authorities in Asheville had little interest in
her shenanigans. The Justice of the Peace said he
had so many other offenses from the passions of the
war to contend with that, since the baby was cared
for and returned, no punishment would be ordered.
It's only that she is freed to the security of your
father. I trust that he won't resent my using his name
since I couldn't promise to be with her all the time
myself.*

*Anymore than I can promise to be with you all the
time. Dear Bethany, I will return at some time to
Falling Water Valley, but it may be a long while, if I
receive further opportunities to hold services in His
name.*

*Again, I encourage you to consider carefully the
only life I can offer you. I will say no more 'til I can
see you again and find out from your own lips (lips I
remember with great tenderness) if you wish me to
ask permission from your father to continue to see
you.*

Until then,
Joshua

Bethany laid the paper on the table without offering to
share it with her father, though she was aware that Nell had
come into the room while she was reading it and that she and
Ben were looking expectantly at her.

Joshua had spoken of asking her father's permission to see
her, but he hadn't spoken of love and he seemed to be trying
to discourage her from really expecting anything to come of
their brief acquaintance.

She tried to control her expression. She wasn't ready to
share her disappointment with them, especially with a strange
boy in the room. She explained quickly that Joshua had been

called away and the situation with Mattie. Speaking of Mattie made her realize that she hadn't come in from caring for Chief. Bethany wondered if she might be feeling uncertain about their reception. With a word of explanation, she hurried out to the stable.

Chief was in the stable along with Rainbow and the bothersome little goat, eating from the food that Mattie had put in his feedbox. He was unharnessed and his coat was dry and smooth. Mattie was gone.

seventeen

There were few places in the small stable where she could be, but Bethany made a cursory search, even though she was certain that Mattie had gone back up the mountain.

Questions and doubt fought with guilt in Bethany's mind. Had Mattie only pretended to repent and seek Christ's peace so that Joshua would send her back to the valley? Could Joshua be fooled so easily? Her emotions plummeted. She had already failed the first mission Joshua had given her. No wonder he had realized that she would never be strong enough to be his helpmate in the calling so dear to him.

In one instant, Bethany made her decision. It was still only late afternoon and there was no snow on the mountain yet. She would go up and confront Mattie as she had the first day that Baby Sally was gone. It became a test in her own mind. If she could get Mattie back down where she would no longer be tempted to pretend mystical abilities, she would be strong enough to share Joshua's life.

She hesitated about telling the others where she was going, then realized that it wouldn't be fair to leave them worrying for several hours. She hurried in and quickly explained the problem to them and snatched up her old cape from her bed.

Nell was as unhappy as she expected, but, surprisingly, her father seemed to understand, only admonishing her not to stay on the mountain so late that she couldn't get back home before dark.

Jimmy offered the observation that Mattie hadn't said more

than three or four words all the time he was bringing her back for Preacher. Obviously thinking that they were all crazy, he announced that he was going to be on his way back to Asheville. As Bethany hurried out the door, Nell was putting several hoecakes into a bit of cloth for him to stuff in his pocket to eat when he made camp for the night.

Chief barely looked up from his feedbox, but Rainbow followed her willingly out of the stable and started swiftly up the mountain after she slipped the horse's bridle on and mounted bareback from a stump.

Though it wasn't snowing yet, the sky was overcast and a chilly wind threw fading leaves about Rainbow's legs and forced Bethany to pull her cape tightly about her as they moved into the bare-limbed trees.

Halfway up the mountain, she saw Mattie's bulk under the too tight brown cloak that Bethany had loaned her just going around a sharp turn in the trail. She urged Rainbow forward and soon overtook her. Seeing them, Mattie moved off the trail and looked as if she were about to disappear into the trees.

"Dear God, give me some of Joshua's wisdom," Bethany whispered.

"Mattie," she called.

Mattie stopped and shrugged off the cloak, thrusting it out toward Bethany. "Here," she said. "It's never covered all of me anyway."

"I don't want the cape back, Mattie. Please wear it. It's chilly up here."

"No," Mattie said stubbornly. "I've got mine back up there." She pointed over her shoulder toward the mountaintop. Her expression told Bethany that an argument over the cloak would be wasted and probably just add to Mattie's obstinacy. Reluctantly, she leaned from Rainbow's back and took the cape, draping it across in front of her.

"Nell has fixed food for you. Please come back."

Mattie stopped and faced her. "I don't belong down there. Nell doesn't like me."

She sounded so like the child that Bethany had seen in her before that she almost smiled. But she decided that she couldn't be less than honest with her.

"Nell has been upset by some of your foolishness in the past, but Joshua's letter said that you have accepted Christ into your heart and you will change your life. You're a child of God now, Mattie. You won't try to fool people that you have special powers anymore. You'll be safer in my home. Safer from temptation to answer people who may come up to get help to find things and safer from valley people who still may be angry about Bertie's baby."

Mattie stood with head bent for a moment and Bethany guessed the confusion going on in her mind. Impulsively, she slipped off Rainbow and took Mattie's hand, feeling the cool hardness of her mountain life still in it.

"Please come back with me, Mattie."

Mattie shook her head stubbornly. "They put me in jail in Asheville. Preacher got me out and let me stay in his sister's house 'til the man saw my case. She was good to me, but I need to get the jail and the town out of me. Preacher said Jesus would always be with me now. Won't He be with me on my mountain?"

"Of course, He will be with you wherever you are, Mattie, but we Christians need each other, too. Especially when we're new Christians."

Mattie didn't drop Bethany's hand, but she didn't move toward the downward trail. "I purely have to go back up my mountain." Her eyes begged Bethany to understand. "I know places no one else knows about. They can't find me."

"We found you."

"Preacher said God guided you to me. I think he might be right."

Sorrowfully, Bethany admitted to herself that she had to give up. If she kept arguing any longer, it would be dark before Mattie got to her mountaintop cabin and she got back home. She held both of Mattie's hands tightly for a moment, then dropped them.

"Mattie, when you're ready, come down to us," she said. "and if it isn't soon, I promise I'll come looking for you. God go with you."

She mounted Rainbow and turned his head toward the valley. A look backwards showed Mattie trudging determinedly up the mountain, dressed in a loose linsey-woolsey dress, undoubtedly furnished by Joshua's sister. All Bethany had managed to do was to take away the warmth of a cloak against the mountain wind.

She thought of Christ's admonition to give your cloak to the person who takes your coat. "I seem to have it backwards, don't I, Jesus?" she whispered.

She didn't try to stop the tears. Surely Joshua was wise not to pursue their attraction. She had just failed the first test God or Joshua had given her. She couldn't honor the request that she keep Mattie with her.

She wasn't worried that the unknown Justice of the Peace in Asheville would care one way or another that Mattie wasn't living under her father's care, but she had failed Joshua.

Joshua's letter was still lying on the table when she stabled Rainbow and went in. She was grateful that her father had respected her privacy and refused to read it. She explained to him that Mattie had been released to his custody since Joshua had to answer a call to preach and wouldn't be back in the valley for some time. Without commenting on Joshua's absence, he agreed with her that the Asheville authorities wouldn't care where Mattie stayed.

After a simple meal, Nell went back to her own home and her father retired to his room, leaving Bethany some badly needed time alone. She was surprised to find that the emotions of the day had left her so exhausted that, after only a short prayer asking forgiveness for her failure with Mattie, she drifted off into a deep and nightlong sleep.

She woke the next morning determined not to give up so easily. After all, Joshua continued to fight for his beliefs without letting failure or even personal danger stop him.

As soon as Nell came to be with Ben, she saddled Rainbow and turned her head up the mountain, not sure of what she would do even if she found Mattie, but feeling that she would keep trying until she talked her back down where she was supposed to be.

"Well, you're starting out early. Now, just who might be sick up there?" Dave Bradley rode his big roan out from a copse of evergreens. Rainbow stopped as the larger animal was pulled in front of her.

"Am I required to explain where I go or who I see?" Bethany answered sharply. She didn't want to explain to anyone what she was trying to do. Certainly not to Dave.

"If it's old Mountaintop Mattie," Dave replied. "Some of us know she came back yesterday and we'd like to know where she is."

Bethany didn't argue the point. She was sure that everyone in the valley knew that Mattie was back, just as they all knew that Joshua had taken her out to Asheville. She decided to appeal to his better side.

"Mattie has changed, Dave. She's accepted Christ. She won't be pretending to have second sight anymore. Please don't do anything to hurt her."

Dave looked at her seriously. "I know I'm not your crusading preacher, Bethany, but I believe in God and I never believed in Mattie's second sight and I don't have any notions to make her pay for taking the baby, though some might. So where is she?"

Bethany hesitated, then answered honestly. "I don't know,

Dave. I'm only looking for her myself."

"Why?" he asked, in obvious confusion. "What can she possibly do for you?"

"I want to do something for her, Dave. She's accepted Christ, but you know new Christians need the support of others. I hope to convince Mattie to come down and live with us."

He looked at her quizzically. "You're afraid to trust her in God's hands?"

Bethany flushed. Even Dave could offer questions that she couldn't answer. It seemed that everywhere she turned she was being told that she didn't know how to be the partner she dreamed of being for Joshua. She twitched Rainbow's reins restlessly, causing her to dance doubtfully on the trail. Perhaps she was being told that the only partner he needed was God.

But there still might be some way she could protect Mattie without bringing her down to the valley. "Dave, if you don't believe in Mattie's powers, why are you looking for her?"

"Down in the church the other night, it was easy to see that you were all caught up in the wandering preacher. Is he coming back?"

"You didn't answer my question."

He pulled his horse closer, almost crowding Rainbow off the trail. "Are you going to answer mine? Do I deserve that much, Bethany?"

She looked into his eyes. He was completely serious. "I don't know."

"Don't know if I deserve that much or if the preacher's coming back?"

She shifted on Rainbow's back. Everything inside her wanted not to have to cope with anything about Dave now.

He seemed to read her discomfort. "I know I've put off serious courting, Bethany, but what I've said to you in jokes, I've meant in my heart. I just," now he showed some discomfort, "didn't want to have you turn me down, so I've waited. I want to know if I've waited too long."

Dear Lord, Bethany prayed, *I've never realized that I could hurt Dave. He's seemed so smart-aleck all the time. Help me answer him now.*

But Dave suddenly pulled his horse off the trail and turned his head down the mountain, not waiting for her to say anything. Was it an answer to her prayer?

"But we'll name all our six children after flowers," he called back, reverting to his old bantering manner.

Bethany let Rainbow have her head on up the mountain. Dave had given her a glimpse of a serious side that he usually covered up. Would Joshua with his deeper insight into his fellow humans have found and encouraged that serious side sooner? How much she had to learn.

Then a sudden realization made her unthinkingly jerk a confused Rainbow to a stop. Dave hadn't answered her question about why he wanted to find Mattie either. Maybe his supposedly serious question was a scheme to keep from answering hers. She patted Rainbow's neck in apology then sent her forward up the trail.

Mattie's cabin was empty and showed no signs that anyone had been in it since Bethany and Joshua had searched it. She wasn't surprised. Mattie would expect her to come searching and probably wouldn't stay in any of the places anyone knew.

Going to the cave would probably be as useless as coming to the cabin. On the chance that Mattie might be listening, she called out that the goat was ready to come back up the mountain.

She couldn't do anything more or accept any more emotion. She turned Rainbow toward the valley and let her pick her own way back to the feedbox.

That night she left the little goat outside the stable. In the morning it was gone. Her father, who had been coerced into drinking its strength-giving milk, expressed satisfaction and Nell admitted that she was tired of milking it.

eighteen

The following weeks brought no word from either Joshua or Mattie. Bethany went up to Mattie's shack on the mountain several times, but she found no indication that Mattie had ever been there. She called out Mattie's name on the possibility that she might be nearby but there was no answer.

One bright day, when the temperature was warm for late November, she put on a sweater, threw her heavy cape behind Rainbow's saddle in case it got cold later and took a lantern up to the waterfall. She stopped Rainbow and dismounted at the spot where Joshua had kissed her. Rainbow stood quietly beside her as she had done that other day, but the absence of Joshua and Chief on the other side of her was as sharp as the sudden wisp of wind that their bodies would have protected her from.

She leaned against Rainbow's bristly flank, letting the sweet memory flood over her until she once again felt the full subtle joining of her being with Joshua that kiss had portended. Then she accepted the pain of Joshua's apology for the kiss. An apology she knew he made from his concern for her. . .but why did it have to be? Why couldn't he stay in the valley and let their love grow slowly and surely as it certainly would?

She pushed herself away from Rainbow and stood looking at the stream, chilly as her own thoughts.

"But what am I doing? Acting as though I'm the only one having to wait for love in this country today? Even in this valley? Is this how I show that I can be a partner for Joshua?"

She bowed her head. "Dear God, forgive me the thoughts I don't always control. I know that You have the first claim on Joshua's life. Whether You bring him back to me or not, please protect him and keep him well."

She moved toward the stream, then stopped. "But, God," she added, "I promise You, I'm going to learn to be strong enough to support him while he does Your work, if You send him back to me."

As though proving her strength, she strode to the waterfall and slipped behind the chilly water, carrying her lantern. There was no light in the cave. She stepped inside and raised the lantern, shivering in the dampness as the air stream met the mist from the waterfall. She realized that going further in would be foolish and senseless. Mattie would never try to spend the winter in the cave. The ledge would ice over when the weather got colder and, unless that other opening was large, Mattie would be trapped inside.

At the thought of ice on the ledge, she turned and almost ran out, as though afraid it would suddenly appear. She was almost past the water when she felt her foot slip. She heard herself scream as she hurtled helplessly through the waterfall and into the stream, landing up to her knees in the frigid water near the bank, still clinging to the lantern as though it might have supported her.

The shock of cold masked any pain she might have felt from the fall and she forced herself not to give in to the panic that pushed against her chest, making it hard to draw in a breath. There was no possibility of drowning. Rainbow stood on the dry land only a few feet away. She struggled to wade toward it, trying to ignore the added chill as the wind slapped her wet skirts against her body.

Some mountain sense and her medical knowledge told her that there might be a risk of having her body temperature dip dangerously low before she got back down the mountain.

"Oh, Mattie, now would be the time for you to appear miraculously with some dry clothes," she muttered. She had a moment of a ridiculous hope that somehow God wasn't watching her get into so much trouble after her brave promise to show how strong she could be. A hope that almost kept her from being willing to pray for the simple strength she would need just to get down the mountain and home.

It lasted only for a moment. If God sometimes understood her more than she wished, He also understood her need and she whispered a prayer even as her shaking hands pulled the voluminous cloak from Rainbow's back. Was it a sign of God's care that she had brought it?

Leaning against the warmth of Rainbow's side, she slipped the wet skirt and petticoat from her shivering body and wrung them out. She slung them beside her saddlebag and wrapped the cloak tightly around herself.

Rainbow stood quietly as usual, apparently not concerned that she rode uncomfortably clinging to the pommel of the saddle and sitting sideways as though it had suddenly turned into a sidesaddle.

Nell and her father were gone when she slipped into the cabin. She dried and warmed herself and was warming her insides with a hot bowl of soup when Nell came in and mentioned that she had chosen a good sunny day to do a bit of washing.

Someday, she silently promised Nell, *I may tell you how I washed those clothes. Someday when I can think of how funny I must have looked bursting through that waterfall instead of how badly I could have been hurt. For now, I'm not going to move from here till you leave.* There was no need to have to explain why she limped like a ninety-year-old with rheumatism.

。。

Word was out in the valley that Mattie was back somewhere

on the mountain, but no one knew where. Nell reported that Bertie was so grateful for getting Baby Sally back that she said she had no desire for revenge and only Dave Bradley's face wore a look of secretiveness whenever Mattie's name was mentioned.

"Let's hope he doesn't find her and try to take revenge or convince her to go back to 'divining'," Nell said to Bethany, when they were working with ginseng roots on the table in Ben's room.

Bethany decided not to mention her own confusion after meeting Dave on the mountain. Since he hadn't attempted to see her again, she felt more than ever unsure about his feelings. Yet she had a nagging thought that she should make him sure that she had no serious sentiments for him. She switched the conversation back to Mattie.

"Why can't I get her to come here where she'll be safe?"

Ben sat by the window watching them. He had recovered enough to see an occasional patient, but still required many rest periods during the day.

"Bethany," he said thoughtfully, "you know that I was very favorably impressed with Joshua, but have you considered that this is the life you'd have to adjust to if you should marry him? You'll spend long months with him gone. You'll have to sometimes accept the pain of losing a convert because, though Christ gives us a new life, we still have free will. Sometimes one of us may choose to go back to the old life, at least temporarily. Perhaps you should consider Dave Bradley's courtship more seriously."

Bethany turned in surprise from the table to look at her father. As a child she used to think that he could read her mind. Now she almost believed it again. A root slipped from her hand and fell to the floor, leaning against her shoe. She didn't notice. But his words clicked something in her mind that had nothing to with Dave Bradley.

"Of course," she whispered shakily. "Of course. This is a taste of what it will be and how strong I must learn to be. But not always in the way I expect it to be." She thought for a moment of her foolish trip back to the cave behind the waterfall and the danger she put herself in. "Joshua didn't know that Mattie would go back up the mountain, but he did keep telling me that I'd have to accept long periods of time without him."

She stood staunchly upright, ignoring the root on her shoe. "I can do it, Daddy. Nell. I am doing it. God knew that I needed to test myself and I'm learning with His help. I'll wait for Joshua when I have to, go with him when I can. Forget about Dave, Daddy."

They were interrupted by a sharp series of knocks on the door. Still in her intense emotional state, Bethany opened it and just managed to repress a surprised gasp. There was still enough light in the day to see Dave Bradley standing there. He wasted no time with any courting talk. half serious or not.

"We've got another raid," he said briefly. "Stay inside 'til you don't hear any more shooting."

He gave Bethany no time to answer but jumped back on his horse and galloped down the valley to the first cabin where he stopped briefly then went on. In spite of his warning, Bethany and Nell hurried out to hide Chief and Rainbow, since Willie was no longer there.

Bethany didn't see any raiders but she saw a flickering fire up on the mountain, blood red against the early evening blackness of the trees.

They were still inside the trees when they saw the horsemen sweep down the mountainside, following old trails that they knew well. Bethany felt a familiar nausea deep inside her, as she thought of the desperately needed food and livestock the valley people were going to lose.

The bushwhackers were in the valley. Afraid to go into the open and praying that the marauders would leave Ben alone,

Nell and Bethany watched helplessly.

Then as the riders slowed at the first cabin down the valley, a warning shot rang out from behind a log near the cabin. It must have come close for the men pushed their horses to a gallop. And, as they rode the length of the valley, shots rang out from hiding places on both sides of the road, 'til the riders faded away in the distance.

Tabitha Ballard was the first one to get to Ben's room where they were quickly filling saddlebags. "You don't need to get out for this one, Doc," she said, gleefully. "Them bushwhackers just found out what a bunch of old men and women and kids can do to protect their homes when they know ahead of time that they're coming."

To their looks of bewilderment, she explained with relish. "Dave Bradley. Him and Mattie. She came to me. . .scared me silly at first. Then she told me about Preacher and what he'd done for her and I believed her that she'd let Jesus change her life. Anyway, she wanted me to get Dave to talk to her and I did. Turned out he was looking for her. You can see what we did. She and Dave agreed on a signal when she saw the bushers coming from the other side of the mountain. Dave made us keep it secret. . .didn't want the bushers to find out. He just told everyone to set up something to hide behind and go there with a gun when he and Dannel rode down the valley yelling out that they were coming."

"Nobody got killed," she continued excitedly, "but some of those old men are still such good shots they made the raiders hear the lead going by their ears. Now we know we can do it, we won't be so scared of the bushwhackers. Maybe they just won't come back to Falling Water Valley."

The ecstatic woman continued talking, but Bethany was no longer listening. So Mattie hadn't turned away from her experience with Jesus. She had found her own way to make up for the bad things she had done in the past. Joshua had brought her to believe that God forgave her but she wanted forgiveness from the valley, too. And now she knew why Dave was looking for Mattie. Not for a bad reason, but for a good one.

And once again, she was learning. God had chosen Dave to help Mattie accomplish her need, instead of herself. Perhaps her attempts to bring Mattie down had been for her own benefit rather than Mattie's. Bethany knew that the tears in her eyes were tears of joy for Mattie and for Joshua. But when would he return to her?

"Please, God, send him back," she prayed.

❧

Dave Bradley appeared at the door one cold morning early in December while Bethany and her father were just finishing their breakfast. He moved to the fire and warmed himself briefly at their invitation but refused Bethany's offer of hot tea.

"Dr. Andrews," he said, approaching Ben formally, standing before him, but looking at Bethany. "I want to ask your permission to call on Bethany."

Bethany jumped, almost dropping the teapot she was holding. Her father put his spoon down and leaned back in his chair, looking as relaxed and thoughtful as if Dave were a patient.

"I think, since Bethany is here, we might as well start with her opinion. You know, Dave, I've always encouraged her to think for herself."

Dave nodded. "We all thought of Bethany as our healing woman while you were gone. She and Nell. Now you're back, she can settle down and be my wife."

Ben stood up. "Dave, I give you permission to talk to Bethany without me and to ask her how she feels about being your wife, but I don't give permission to call on her unless she gives you permission."

With this somewhat muddled expression, he walked to the

door to his room and closed it forcefully behind him.

Dave turned to Bethany and took the teapot from her hands, setting it carefully on the table.

"Bethany, it isn't likely that preacher is coming back here. I told you that day on the mountain that I've been patient and I have. But I don't want you to get laughed at here in the valley. Most everyone knows you were really sweet on him. You somehow showed it that night at the church. I'm going out to get in the war, Bethany, but if we let them know that we're courtin' serious before I go, they'll think you forgot him."

Bethany looked at him in surprise. "Do you mean you're asking to call on me just to keep me from being laughed at?"

He hesitated, then grinned. "Well, yes, I guess I am."

Bethany relaxed. At this moment when she was about to turn Dave down forever, she liked him better than at any other time. She touched his hand and shook her head.

"That's about the nicest thing anyone ever did for me, Dave, but it isn't necessary. The people of the valley are my friends. I don't worry about them laughing at me."

Did Dave look relieved? "And you're going to wait for the preacher?"

Bethany hesitated. There was no need to answer him. He already knew. "I'll pray for you, Dave, if you do enlist. Everyone in the valley will. We all appreciate what you and Mattie have done for us."

Dave shrugged. "Tabitha has set up a schedule for the men to go up on the mountain each day while Mattie sleeps and for the women to watch for the signal. Maybe they can keep the men from turning their guns on each other after they chase the bushwhackers off."

After a few more words, they parted as friends. Bethany briefly explained to her father, who merely smiled.

nineteen

Joshua was feeling tired and depressed in spite of the beauty of the snow-covered mountains he was riding through. He was cold, feeling every twinge of a north wind that seemed to get inside his long coat, as he rode toward Asheville.

The request to hold a camp meeting that he had been responding to when he sent Mattie back to Falling Water Valley had led to a good beginning with people pathetically eager to hear the gospel preached again. But on the third night, the word had gone out about the preaching. A group of armed men galloped into the clearing where he was holding services and scattered the congregation into hiding in the trees. After that, they were afraid to come back. Though he had appeared at the clearing for the next two days, no one came.

He rode over by Knoxville and each night gathered a few that he thought were faithful into a church. A heavy snow became an excuse for them to not return.

Christmas was near. He determined to visit his sister in Asheville, where any request for his services would have been left. If there was none he would go back to Falling Water Valley for Bethany's decision. But he had little reason to expect anything but a "No" from Bethany and her father. What did he have to offer a wife but loneliness and hardship?

He was even afraid to pray that Bethany would agree to share his life, for if she should not be strong enough to accept it, she might find only unhappiness. He only prayed for what would be best for her.

He had to force himself to look up and repeat the words, "I will lift up mine eyes unto the hills, from whence cometh my help. My help cometh from the Lord, which made heaven and earth. He will not suffer thy foot to be moved; he that keepeth thee will not slumber." (Psalm 121: 1-3)

But the words and the beauty of the tree-covered mountains brought him comfort. After looking up, he looked down at the horse under him. Impulsively, he leaned forward and patted the horse's neck.

"Old Solomon, I'll never know how you made your way back to the stable in Asheville after I was pulled off your back and beaten to a pulp, but I thank God for you."

The horse picked up his head and whinnied. For a minute Joshua thought he was responding to his words, then he realized that a rider was coming down the road toward him. The other rider pulled off the road into the heavy bushes, leaving tracks in the snow.

Joshua pulled Old Solomon to a stop and called out his usual greeting, "God's peace, to you, friend." It was not only a blessing but it indicated that he was a minister, not carrying arms.

The rider, who sat his horse well and whose good-looking boots showed beneath a long homespun coat, slowly pulled his horse into the road and Joshua had a momentary flash of recognition. But it faded as he tried to remember where he had seen the man.

"Joshua Holt?" The man called, holding his hands out to show that he had no gun in them, though Joshua could see a long barrel strapped to the bedroll behind him.

Joshua, remembering that the bushwhackers who had beaten him also knew him by sight, remained alert to trouble. But, as he always tried to do, he gave the man the benefit of the doubt and acknowledged his own identity.

"They told me in Asheville to look for you around Knox-ville. This is a lucky meeting. I'm carrying a call for you to come preach."

Joshua tried to stop the downward swoop of his emotions. "God, I accept Your word that I shouldn't go back to Falling Water Valley," he whispered.

Then he answered the man. "Wherever it is, I'll come. Will you give me directions?"

"You know the way, Preacher. The people of Falling Water Valley remember your sermon, and they want you to open their church for at least one meeting. Christmas Day." The man hesitated. "It's the women who're asking," he added, with a serious expression. "You may not find all the men so ready to listen to you again."

Joshua had a struggle with his breath. A definite reason to go to Falling Water Valley. He was momentarily too affected even to be able to form a thankful prayer.

The rider pulled his horse alongside and held out his hand. "I'm Dave Bradley."

Joshua took his hand even as he remembered the man who stood up and denounced him at the emotion-packed session at the church.

Dave didn't offer an apology and Joshua had no intention of asking for one. Instead he asked about Mattie.

A faint flicker of a grin flashed across Dave's face. "There's a few people in the valley who complain about your influence with Mattie, but most of them would rather have what she's doing now than her make-believe second sight."

Dave told him about Mattie and the defenses the men and women of the valley had put into practice.

"You haven't asked me about Dr. Andrews and Bethany," Dave added, a quizzical look on his face. He waited for Joshua's response, not offering any information on his own.

"Of course I do want to know about them," Joshua admitted.

"Dr. Andrews is all well now. He's back to practice in the valley and riding out to other communities. It's been a long time since there's been a real doctor around. He's gone for several days at a time, pretty much." He hesitated a minute then added, "He'll make sure to be at home when you're there. He and Nell will probably ask you to marry them."

Joshua nodded, not surprised. He edged Old Solomon closer and looked Dave full in the face. "And Bethany?" He didn't try to pretend that the answer wasn't important to him.

"She's busy. She and Nell still try to take Ben's place while he's gone." He looked away.

Joshua waited quietly for him to continue. Would he be asked to marry this man to Bethany? Was that one of the reasons he was seeking out a minister?

But Dave pulled his horse back and headed him around Old Solomon. He seemed to have said all he intended to about Bethany.

"Now that I've helped the valley to learn to defend themselves, I'm going to get into the fighting. I promised to find you and deliver the call. Now that I've done it, I'll be on my way. I want to find a place to stay before night. It's too cold to sleep out. Oh," he called back, "I almost forgot . . .Tabitha Ballard sends an invite to stay with them while you're there. She thinks it wouldn't be meet for you to stay at Dr. Andrews."

Joshua noticed that he didn't specify which army and chose not to ask him or respond to his delivery of the invitation.

"God's blessings on you," he called.

The man raised a hand in salutation as he pulled his horse onto the road and took off in a fast trot.

Joshua kept Old Solomon standing for a moment as he bowed his head in prayer. "My Lord, I thank You for Your goodness."

Then he forced himself to keep the horse at a fast walk. It was too late to start toward Falling Water Valley before dark and he continued toward Asheville. He noticed that the wind had stopped, but he chided himself for his impression that it had suddenly become warmer.

"Just the same," he reminded himself, "I mustn't push Bethany. It was such a short time together. she may well have forgotten any feelings for me, and almost certainly doesn't have enough to be willing to accept the only life I can offer."

He pulled Old Solomon up to his sister's small frame house in Asheville just before dark. It was the house he grew up in and Joshua always had an emotional feeling of coming home when he saw it.

He slipped off the horse and was in the process of stretching his complaining muscles when ten-year-old Sammy hit his midsection like a happy little catapult. Joshua caught himself in mid-stagger and reached down to hug the little boy whose arms were clutching his waist in a loving embrace.

"First I thought you were Daddy. Then I knew it was you. Can I put Old Solomon away for you? Mommy made lots of soup today. Did anybody come with you? Mommy said to just come on in. There was a man here looking for you."

"Whoa, Sammy. Your tongue is going to get tired." Joshua tightened his arms lovingly around his only nephew. "I met the man on the road. Yes, you can put up Solomon. Be sure he's dry."

Sammy unwrapped himself and just gave Joshua a look that scorned any suggestion that he wouldn't rub Solomon down before feeding him. Joshua gave him a final hug and went into his sister's cozy living room.

She was waiting for him in the doorway to the kitchen with a ladling spoon in her hand. Joshua thought how symbolic of his sister's attitude toward the world: Given the power, she would feed it. The greatest sorrow she and John Wright had was that Sammy was their only child. Since he was, June spent her extra maternal tenderness on those she thought needed it, starting with her brother.

She hardly took time to hug him before she had his boots off, and he was sitting in the kitchen before her warm cookstove with his cold feet resting on the open door of the tiny oven, smelling the almost-forgotten aroma of real coffee. Soon he had a cup of the dark ambrosia in his hand.

"Oh, I think of this kitchen whenever I'm cold," he said. "It's even better than the fireplace."

"Sammy thinks so," she said. "And," she added, "I hope you noticed that you are drinking real coffee."

Joshua grinned. "I noticed and I love it but I thought maybe it might be better not to mention it."

June's plump face frowned mightily at him as she rubbed her hands on her spotless apron. "Joshua Holt, you know that I wouldn't use contraband coffee, what with John off fighting for the Confederacy. I've saved this for special times."

"What's special about me coming here this time, except the possibility that some of John's friends will denounce you for continuing to harbor someone who preaches against slavery and the war?" Joshua spoke seriously. He and his brother-in-law had always been good friends, but it had been a shock to him when John left his family to fight for the South.

June stood for a minute with a bowl in her hand. Then she set it on the checkered tablecloth and hustled over to hug him again.

"They grant me you. Several Southern sympathizers came here to tell me that they had nothing to do with the beating you took and they condemned it powerfully. But, Joshua, you know that I have to support my husband, no matter what you or I think."

"Of course, June. I don't judge you. . .or him."

June busied herself filling a huge tureen with a thick venison soup, talking as she worked. Joshua reflected that Sammy may have inherited his busy tongue from her. She acknowledged Sammy's entrance into the front room with a faint smile but didn't stop talking to Joshua.

"Lucky that I'm making corn pone or you'd have to take your feet out of the oven to let me bake bread. And have you heard from Mattie? I can't tell you how much I'm in awe at what you and Jesus did for her. Jimmy said she went back with him and he gave your letter to Bethany. When do I get to meet Bethany? Jimmy said she's pretty. You can come to the table now. It's ready. Bring your coffee cup. I have a little more in the pot. Sammy, come on in and wash up. Are you sure you took good care of Old Solomon? Be sure to wash up now."

Grinning, Joshua and Sammy followed her directions. Joshua waited until he had said grace before answering her questions.

"June," he chided, gently, "you know you are only awed by what Jesus did for Mattie. Don't put me first."

"Did I say you first? I ask forgiveness. Now tell me about Mattie. . .and Bethany."

"I haven't heard directly from them, but I met a man on the road who carried a message for me to come to hold a Christmas service there."

"Oh, I hoped you were going to spend Christmas here." June's pleasant face showed disappointment for a moment. Then she brightened. "But I'm glad you're going back to Bethany."

"June, I may have talked too much about Bethany. Since I've had more time to consider, I know that she and her father will probably not think well of my poor qualifications as a husband. Look at the life I'd offer her. A life of waiting for me to come home while I follow my calling."

"A lot of women are waiting for their men to come home now," June said seriously. "We don't regret having married our husbands."

"But you look forward to the end of the war and your husband's return. Bethany wouldn't. No, June, I'm convinced that I've been rightly determined not to marry. I can't put Bethany to such a test."

"Sammy, if you're through eating you can be excused to finish your arithmetic lesson."

June waited until Sammy had reluctantly gone into the other room. "Are you saying, then, Joshua, that you were wrong about thinking you love Bethany?"

"No, never. I love her."

"But you'll go to Falling Water Valley and never declare yourself to her? Mama, forgive me, how I've failed you with my little brother." June placed her spoon in her bowl and looked dramatically up to the ceiling.

In spite of the seriousness of the discussion, Joshua had to laugh. Then he sobered.

"The call to Falling Water Valley didn't come from Bethany or her father. Dave Bradley said it was the idea of the women in the valley. They remember that one unplanned service and long for another on Christmas Day."

"So you'll be leaving again in a few days?"

"Yes. There's something I want to do for Bethany." He explained about the sad condition of the cemetery and how it disturbed Bethany.

"I want to get the people of the valley to do as good a job of clearing the cemetery as we can in the winter weather. If we can work together on that and, at least some of them come together for a church service, maybe I can leave a little bit of peace there. If the snow stays on, we may not be able to do much of anything. I'm hoping for a warmer spell. Sometimes it happens in December."

June looked fiercely at him. "I plan to pray a lot."

She didn't indicate if she planned to pray about the weather or his decision about Bethany. Joshua decided not to ask her about it.

"Now," she said decisively, "you look like a good long night in bed is just what you need. It's always ready for you."

Joshua didn't argue. Relaxation and warmth had made him realize just how tired he was. He was asleep as soon as he felt the feather bed under him.

twenty

It was coming home. Even more than arriving at his sister's house in Asheville, entering this valley where he had spent a few crowded days was coming home. Joshua stopped Old Solomon at the mouth of the lane leading down to the church.

The blackberry bushes where he had been half hidden when Bethany found him were barely visible now against the strips of dark earth showing through scant patches of snow. Thinking of his rescue, Joshua bowed his head for a moment in prayer for the safe return of the boy-man who had helped Bethany then ran off to war rather than keep his secret from his parents.

"Father, please let me take his hand and give him Your blessing in some future time of peace."

He sat motionless on Old Solomon for awhile then turned the horse's head toward the church. It looked as empty and desolate as though the dramatic evening when the baby was returned had never happened. Morosely, he accepted the humility of realizing that his sermon that night had made little difference in the community.

Weeds and grasses that were allowed to grow up around the church only showed the effects of nature's freezing and thawing; no scythe had been laid to them. Depressed, he swung off the horse and walked over the wet ground to the cemetery.

It looked the same. The tall grass was softened and drooping by snow and thaw. It would be harder to cut than if they had done it in the fall but, standing there, he determined, with the help of God, to bring these people out here to honor the last resting place of their own ancestors. Whether it was his gift to Bethany, who grieved for the neglected cemetery, or a small way of bringing the community together in one common effort, it must be tried.

"A lot of sunshine, Father, will be appreciated before Christmas Eve."

He mounted Old Solomon and guided him out to the road leading up to Dr. Andrews' cabin nestled among trees against the mountain at the end of the valley.

It was Nell who saw him coming. She was in the big room cutting potatoes taken from a straw-filled cache near the barn for soup.

"Rider coming," she called out to Bethany, through the open door to the office room. "Looks familiar." She was silent for a moment as Bethany didn't answer and the rider came closer. "Looks real familiar."

Bethany appeared in the doorway, looking at Nell rather than toward the road.

"Not Dave?"

"Not Dave. Heard that Dave shook the dust of the valley off forever. Rode out to somewhere. Left a certain woman who didn't appreciate him. Not Ben either. Come look."

Could it be? Bethany moved over beside Nell, afraid to look. Afraid to breathe. She focused her gaze on the porch first, then finally on the man who had halted his horse. . .was that Old Solomon? . . .and was swinging long legs to the ground. . .Joshua. Joshua was here.

On the verge of running out to meet him, she stopped. He had stayed away for nearly two months with no word, except the letter sent back with Mattie. And that letter had haunted her. It had come so close to asking her to forget him. Yet she had spent the time since he left refusing to forget him but trying to grow strong enough to adjust her life to his great commission.

How should she greet him now?

Nell, with her sensitive awareness of Bethany's confusion, went to the front door of the cabin to welcome Joshua.

"Come in. Come in," she cried. "Good to see you looking so healthy. What a change from the first time I saw you."

Joshua grinned, walking across the porch and entering the room. "Still the healer, Nell. Checking out my health before I even get in the house."

He spoke to Nell but his eyes were on Bethany, standing as if paralyzed, both hands flat on the table.

Nell stepped back, ushering him through the door. He strode across the floor to stand beside Bethany. Gently, he lifted her hands from the table and held them in his.

At his touch, something in Bethany's mind remembered the feel of being in his arms, a memory so strong she almost felt that she was there now. She pulled herself back from the memory.

"But your hands are so cold," she heard herself saying. "Come over to the fire and warm them. We've had snow and cold but it seemed to be warming up today. But your hands are so cold it must not be. . ."

She realized that senseless words were bubbling out of her mouth and stopped in mid-sentence. What would he make of her repeated comments on the coldness of his hands?

Joshua dropped her hands and moved as she suggested to the fireplace. She only felt the chill in his hands, not the warmth he so wanted to feel in her response to his coming. He had asked her to consider carefully if she wanted to accept his courtship and she had answered him.

Nell, looking as if she wanted to give both of them a good shaking, interrupted the awkward silence with a happy announcement of her own.

"Pastor, Ben and I have been hoping for you. We have a request."

Joshua turned from the fireplace, a relieved and affectionate look in his eyes. "Could it possibly be to perform a marriage ceremony?"

Nell grinned. "It could. Ben should be back tonight. Where are you staying?"

"With Tabitha and Nathan Ballard. She sent the invitation along with the call to preach in the church on Christmas Day."

Bethany stiffened. So he hadn't come back to see her. But why hadn't she known about Tabitha's request? Nell asked the question she couldn't find words for.

"We didn't know. Who took the request to you?"

Again, Joshua answered Nell but looked at Bethany. "Dave Bradley. He was on his way to join the fighting."

Nell nodded. "We knew that. But why didn't Tabitha tell us you were coming?"

"She and a few other women decided to keep the call secret from the men. I'm not sure why she kept it from you."

Joshua left them soon, saying that he needed to get Old Solomon cared for and into shelter at Tabitha's stable before the horse became chilled. But before he left, they agreed that the marriage of Ben and Nell would take place in the church immediately after services on Christmas Day.

"It will help to bring people into the service," Joshua said. "And I hope to get some of the community to clean up the cemetery on Christmas Eve. A fire will burn the debris and help keep us warm."

He wanted to say to Bethany that it was his desire to give that to her as his gift, but he mustn't place any sort of pressure on her to reconsider his courtship.

Watching him ride off, Bethany could only be grateful for the happy task of getting ready for the wedding ceremony.

❧

"I get a funny feeling cleaning up the graveyard on Christmas

Eve," Tabitha Ballard said to Bethany. "Usually it's in spring and fall. . .and just a little warmer than this."

She stopped talking for a minute while she and Bethany worried at a stubborn root with their hoes.

"But," she added thoughtfully, "Preacher's right. We can't have a Christmas service in the church with the graves of our ancestors lying untended out here."

Bethany smiled, looking toward the place where Joshua, with his coat off, chopped at several small saplings which had taken advantage of the neglect to take root beside a grave.

She had hardly talked with him since he had ridden up to the cabin two days ago. She was still disappointed at their awkward first meeting and at learning that he had come in response to a request by some of the women of the valley to conduct a Christmas day service in the church rather than to see her. Yet she was deeply glad for the service and the wedding of her father and Nell afterwards.

"We only told Dave we wanted him to come," Tabitha said, "because we were afraid that Preacher might not be able to come, or our men would refuse to allow it if they had time to think about it." She grinned shyly at Bethany. "We didn't tell you because we weren't sure how you felt about Preacher. . . and so soon after Dave leaving. . ."

Her unfinished sentence invited Bethany to share those feelings, but Bethany put the hoe down and knelt to wrestle the root with her bare hands, glad for the excuse not to meet Tabitha's brightly curious eyes.

Would he have come, Bethany wondered, just to see her? She couldn't tell by his attitude. He had spent his nights with Tabitha and Nathan Ballard. And he seemed to be treating her with the same Christian friendliness that he showed for all the other members of the Falling Water Valley church.

She pulled the root with a final jerk and changed the subject with Tabitha. "We're just lucky that it warmed up enough to melt off the snow here in the graveyard. And, you have to admit that the dampness makes it easier to get these roots out."

Tabitha grunted. "You can call it damp. I call it mud."

"I'm thinking Doc is going to have a busy time after this." Virgie Smith had come up behind them and overheard their last remarks. "But maybe it's worth it," she added, looking at the busy scene in front of them. "Almost everyone in the valley has come out. They may not all admit that they yearn for church like we do, but at least we're remembering our dead out here the way we once did."

"Bertie MacMillan didn't come. She couldn't bring herself to leave Baby Sally in the church with the other little ones," Tabitha said. "It reminds her too much of that horrible night that she was stolen."

"We all have to understand that," Virgie agreed.

"Oh, no." Tabitha straightened up and pointed excitedly toward the middle of the cemetery. "Bethany, look!"

Bethany's gaze followed her pointing finger, to rest in suspense on two men. Clyde MacMillan and Carl Dietz stood beside the graves where their respective ancestors had been buried side by side, as they had lived as neighbors, many years before the war.

Each of the men, wielding scythes, had cleared off the graves of their own families, and each, Bethany realized with dismay, had carefully cleared a grave-shaped space beside them. Almost as if she could enter into their minds, she knew they acted in hopes of someday getting back the bodies of their dead sons, one Union, one Confederate.

Now they faced each other across the high grasses that separated the cleared spaces, sharpened curves of the scythes held out threateningly toward each other. Bethany wanted to shout for Joshua, who was helping carry the saplings to the edge of the forest, but even her throat seemed to be paralyzed. She felt something that was almost nausea flash through her body.

Was the war going to push its evil even here where they had gathered with hopes of some healing coming from the care of their family graves? Would this day end in the death of one or both of those men? In a murder?

She realized that others in the cemetery and men who were swinging their own scythes around the church building, had stopped working to watch the men. They seemed as stricken by paralysis as she was. They stood as if helplessly waiting for the tragedy that would split their valley even more. It was as though the earth and everything on it had stopped around the two men.

Only Sophie Dietz, who had turned and seen the threat to her husband, uttered a low moan. Bravely moving into the tall grass between the two men, she dropped to her knees. The grasses rustled gently from the movement of her sturdy body. Everything else was still.

Then three other women stepped into the grass. Led by Tabitha, one by one they silently joined Sophie on their knees between the angry men.

Clyde MacMillan moved first. Lowering his scythe to ground level, he cut a swath that took down about a fourth of the high grass between them, coming dangerously close to the women. Then he turned away without speaking and walked toward the edge of the graveyard.

Carl Dietz watched him until he was in the lane leading out toward the road. Then he caught Sophie's hand and helped her up. When she and the other women had moved out of the way, he scythed down the rest of the grass, including the uncut grass over the space where Clyde MacMillan's little grand-daughter would someday rest.

Sophie reached out to touch him, but he shook her hand off and walked toward the trees, in the opposite direction from the one Clyde MacMillan had taken.

Bethany didn't try to hold back the tears. The aversion of

the tragedy that seemed so close to being played out, Clyde's refusal to hurt the brave women who stepped forth, was a shadowy sign of the possibility of some future healing in the valley.

She watched as Joshua came back into the graveyard and listened to the excited stories of what had happened. He put his arm around Sophie's shoulder and let her cry. In a short time she stood back and, after a few words with Joshua, she, too, left the cemetery.

The workers were quieter, but seemed to be working harder, and they soon had all the churchyard looking as good as it had in earlier days.

"It's good," Tabitha said, almost to herself, "but in the old days we would have had dinner on the grounds after we finished."

She and Bethany watched the neighbors leave, still gathering in groups together with those who agreed with their attitude toward the war.

"It's not the same," Tabitha said. "But," she smiled and squeezed Bethany's hand, "we're going to have Christmas services tomorrow. And a wedding, bless Doc and Nell and praise God." Waving, she followed the people out to the road.

Bethany looked around. For a minute, she thought that she and Joshua were the only ones left in the churchyard and, ignoring the chill she felt in her damp feet, she hoped for a time to talk.

Then she saw Mattie. She was hunched over a space at the edge of the graveyard. From where she stood, Bethany could just make out two barely raised mounds there. She swallowed her disappointment and followed Joshua to stand beside her. Mattie was wearing her deerskin cape but her hair was put up in a bun. She was down on her knees.

She looked up at Joshua. She seemed to be unaware of the wet chill of the mud under her knees. She pointed toward a sandstone rock that she had placed between the graves.

"Preacher, I brought this down to mark their graves," she said, without any greeting. "I need help. I've got a knife, but I can't make their names on it."

Without forcing a greeting from her, Joshua accepted that she meant she couldn't read or write. Bethany watched as he carefully scratched the names of her father and mother on the rock. Mattie didn't know their birth and death dates, so he carved in approximate ones.

Joshua touched Mattie's shoulder. "You've forgiven them, then?"

Mattie nodded. Bethany, knowing that they were referring to discussions that she hadn't been a part of, stepped back a bit, in case they wanted to talk more.

But Joshua pulled her into a circle with Mattie to offer prayers. Then, without further talk, Mattie turned away and soon disappeared up some secret trail to her beloved mountain-top.

"Some of the men have gone up and built her a real cabin in thanks for her acting as a sentry for the bushwhackers," Bethany explained to Joshua, as they watched her go.

At last they were alone. But did Joshua want to be alone with her? It seemed as if he had tried to keep other people between them ever since he rode into the valley. Now there was no one to come between them. If he chose not to talk about their love, she would know that his feelings for her hadn't been deep enough to last during their separation, while she was learning her own strengths.

She started to walk away, expecting him to follow her. Instead, he caught her hand and turned her to face the church with him.

twenty-one

"Bethany, I told you once that I thanked God for the beating that left me here and brought you to me." He stopped and stood quietly, not looking at Bethany or forcing her to look at him. If she wanted to ignore his reference to their feelings for each other, he would make her free to do it.

Bethany waited. His observation seemed unfinished. Did he still give thanks or was he trying to tell her gently that she must forget him?

As he didn't add anything further, she dropped his hand and started again to walk off. She didn't want to hear the rest of what he would say. She only wanted to get somewhere where she could be alone to cry.

He watched her move off and made no attempt to stop her. If he could say "No" to his calling and his need to travel for God, he would pursue this beautiful woman with all his being. But, even in his pain, he had to offer up to God first place in his life. And he had to understand Bethany's choice not to share that life. He bowed his head.

Bethany plunged ahead, her tears blotting out any sight of the lane where she was walking, only anxious to get to the road and, as soon as possible, up to her cabin.

A sudden gust of cold wind slapped against her face. It seemed to shut off her breath and turn her tears to ice. The chill of it on her face added to her mental distress, became physical pain.

Automatically, she pulled her cape tightly about her shoulders and turned away from it. And found herself looking at Joshua, standing with bowed head before the church.

She didn't stop to think whether his feelings for her had changed or not. Only that he was alone and needed comfort. She turned and ran back.

He lifted his head and held out his arms to her, the joy in his face telling her more surely than any words of his deep love. As he enfolded her in his arms and pressed his mouth to hers, she knew that here was home, no matter where they might be.

❧

The church was filled with the nose-niggling scent of cast iron heating up after a long period of being cold. Someone had split hickory logs and piled enough into the little potbellied stove below the pulpit to make only the back of the church chilly while the temperature in the front rose to an August warmth.

Though the church was far from crowded, Bethany didn't try to guess whether there was a fair-sized gathering for services on Christmas Day because the valley people wanted to hear Joshua's sermon or because they wanted to see their doctor marry their old friend Nell.

It didn't matter. She was just happy that they were there. She slipped into the back pew so she could revel in the sight of them; Nell sat on the front pew on the women's side looking as composed as though her life wasn't to be changed in a beautiful way in a short while. Bethany looked to where her father sat in a similar pew on the men's side and smiled. Dr. Ben Andrews was twisting about like a nervous child, looking over to Nell as frequently as a child looks at whoever is his anchoring person. Bethany thought that the heightened color in his face may have been from more than the effects of his nearness to the stove.

She let her gaze wander over the rest of the congregation. On the women's side, Virgie Smith sat beside Bertie MacMillan, ready to help her keep the sleepy Baby Sally quiet. She spotted Annie Bowers, sitting with bowed head and remembered that there had been no word from young Willie since he left the day they found Joshua. Sophie Dietz, who knew her son was dead, sat behind her.

For a moment, Bethany struggled again with her feelings of guilt. Then she put it into a prayer for Willie's safety. He had been determined to get into the fighting. Though her caution not to tell anyone about Joshua may have sent him out a few days sooner, it wasn't the reason for his going.

She turned her gaze to Maude MacNeil, who was giving up the battle with young Jamie and letting him slip across the aisle to sit with his father on the men's side of the church, where it seemed many of the men of the valley had decided to come to the service. Carl Dietz sat next to the wall in a seat near the front while Clyde MacMillan sat on the aisle on a back pew, as though they consciously or unconsciously sat as far apart as possible.

Turning back to the women's side, Bethany was surprised that Tabitha Ballard sat away from everyone on a bench just in front of herself. That was unusual for the sociable Tabitha. But perhaps she simply wanted to be alone with her thoughts in this service that she had requested.

But for Bethany, even more than for the rest of the assemblage, the focus was on the tall man who stood behind the pulpit, resting both hands on his open Bible and looking over the people with a happiness that softened his handsome face. Joshua was waiting serenely for them to settle down. . .or for something else. Bethany felt as if they were already so much one that she could pick up even his need for something. . . what?

Her question was answered suddenly as the door opened hesitantly and a carefully groomed Mattie slipped in as quietly as her bulk allowed. Tabitha turned with a proud smile and beckoned to her to take the space beside herself.

Bethany looked back at Joshua's pleased face as he prepared to start the service now that Mattie completed the congregation. She pushed down her returning disappointment that God had chosen Tabitha Ballard and Dave Bradley as the ones to help Mattie change her image in the valley and keep her changed life intact instead of herself.

She remembered her earlier certainty that the only way she could prove her ability to be Joshua's helpmate was to bring Mattie down to her cabin. Now, she realized that accepting God's better plan for Mattie and her own lack of involvement in it was also a lesson on her path to learning how to take her place by Joshua's side. Her prayer of thanks for the lesson was still hard to whisper. *We never reach perfection, do we? Did God smile?*

She smiled as she settled back to listen to Joshua's service. After several rousing Christmas carols that put the congregation into nostalgic memories of happier Christmases, Joshua read them Luke's always new story of Christ's birth.

His sermon took them back to that unhappy and frightening period in the land of Israel when the greatest event of all time came to pass. He didn't berate them for their own anger with each other or try to give meaning to emotions that often overwhelmed them but led them gently to hope for a future time of peace.

The service ended with a soft singing of "Silent Night." Bethany thought she saw tears in some eyes which still refused to meet those of former friends.

Then Joshua motioned for Ben and Nell to stand with him beside the pulpit and invited the congregation to witness their marriage. No one left until he had performed the simple ceremony that joined them as man and wife.

But even as the people crowded forward, laughing and half crying to shake the hands of Preacher and of the new couple, she saw Clyde MacMillan hurry out, followed by a few others who left without wishing them well, rather than risk meeting face-to-face with their own sworn enemies. There would be no gathering up in the cabin at the head of the valley as there would have been in the old days.

Bethany tried not to notice as she took advantage of her own turn to fling her arms around Nell, rest happily in her father's arms for a moment, then feel both her hands come home, clasped in Joshua's.

ಶಿ

Bethany sat beside the fireplace in her room, too excited for the moment to clear away the dishes from the meal that she and Joshua had shared with her father and Nell. Nell had gone down to her own cabin to put together the few things she would bring up to Ben's room. Joshua and Ben had retired to his room where Bethany knew he would ask her father for permission to marry her.

She wasn't concerned that her father would do anything but give them his blessing. She just felt that she couldn't wait any longer for Joshua to come back in and take her in his arms. Then would come a time of planning.

She ran to meet him when he came in from the other room. He took both her hands in his, then pulled her close inside his arms, and held her there for a moment, just letting his gaze caress her face. His broad grin seemed to celebrate everything that had happened since the gust of wind had spun her around toward him.

"Dr. Andrews logically reminded me of how short our acquaintance is, but he understands and accepts our love for each other."

She pressed her head into the hollow of his shoulder. They just held each other for awhile, being happy. Then Joshua lifted her head from his shoulder and continued.

"And, if we hold to our feelings for each other, he will give you into my hands at some future time."

He looked solemn. "I don't know at what future time, my love. It can't be 'til this war is over. I can't have you in the danger that brought me in here."

He gently moved her to arm's length and looked deeply into her eyes, as though to be sure that everything was open and clear with them. "Bethany, you know that I have to keep on with my calling to be a circuit rider. Much as I love you, I must put my devotion to God first."

Bethany raised her gaze to answer his. "I've been on the move most of my life, Joshua. And those people you'll be preaching to will need some of my medicine, too."

She closed her eyes and, grasping his hands, pulled his arms back around her, feeling them tighten about her. She spoke from their warmth.

"There's going to be such a lot of healing needed all over the South, when this war is over. Physical healing as well as emotional. So much healing is needed right here in Falling Water Valley. Maybe God will send you back here. Let's just let it be up to Him. But wherever you go, Joshua, whenever it may be that we can marry, I promise you this. . ." Bethany opened her eyes and let Joshua see the love blazing there, as she paraphrased Ruth's promise, "I'll go where you go, or I'll keep a home for you to return to, whichever serves God and you best."

A Letter To Our Readers

Dear Reader:

In order that we might better contribute to your reading enjoyment, we would appreciate your taking a few minutes to respond to the following questions. When completed, please return to the following:

Rebecca Germany, Managing Editor
Heartsong Presents
P.O. Box 719
Uhrichsville, Ohio 44683

1. Did you enjoy reading *Falling Water Valley?*
   ❑ Very much. I would like to see more books
     by this author!
   ❑ Moderately
     I would have enjoyed it more if _____

   _____

2. Are you a member of **Heartsong Presents**? ❑Yes ❑No
   If no, where did you purchase this book? _____

   _____

3. What influenced your decision to purchase this
   book? (Check those that apply.)

   ❑ Cover   ❑ Back cover copy

   ❑ Title   ❑ Friends

   ❑ Publicity   ❑ Other_____

4. How would you rate, on a scale from 1 (poor) to 5
   (superior), the cover design? _____

5. On a scale from 1 (poor) to 10 (superior), please rate the following elements.

    ___Heroine   ___Plot

    ___Hero   ___Inspirational theme

    ___Setting   ___Secondary characters

6. What settings would you like to see covered in **Heartsong Presents** books?_____

_____

_____

7. What are some inspirational themes you would like to see treated in future books?_____

_____

_____

8. Would you be interested in reading other **Heartsong Presents** titles? ❏ Yes   ❏ No

9. Please check your age range:
   ❏ Under 18   ❏ 18-24   ❏ 25-34
   ❏ 35-45   ❏ 46-55   ❏ Over 55

10. How many hours per week do you read? _____

Name _____

Occupation _____

Address _____

City_____ State_____ Zip _____

WHEN I'M ON MY KNEES

Anita Corrine Donihue

Prayers especially for women, prayers that emanate from
the heart, prayers that deal with friendship, family, and
peace. Packaged in a beautifully printed leatherette cover,
women will also find hymns and poems that focus
on prayer in their everyday lives.

About the author:
Anita Corrine Donihue, a teacher with thirty years
of experience, is the coauthor of *Apples for a Teacher*
and *Joy to the World,* two very popular titles
from Barbour Books.

(212 pages, Leatherette, 4" x 6¾")